PLAYING
FOR KEEPS
in Half Moon Bay

KATIE O'CONNOR

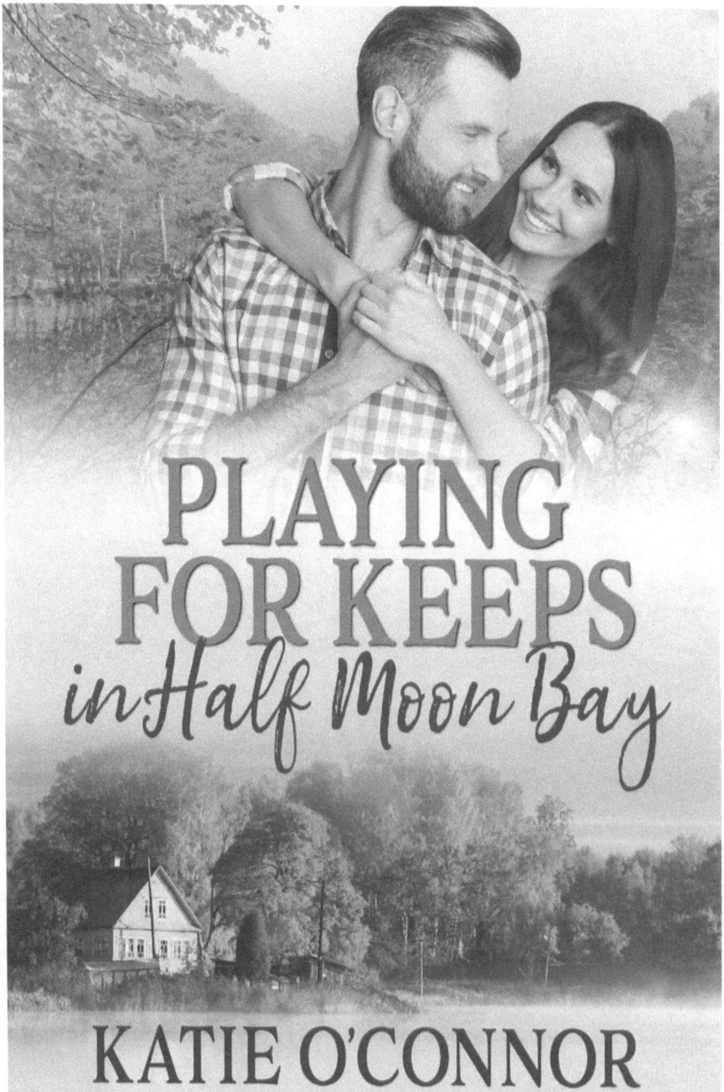

Playing for Keeps in Half Moon Bay

A Bellamie Brothers of Half Moon Bay Novel

Katie O'Connor

Dedication

This one is for all the people who have touched my life in small ways.

Especially Lori McLean, Loretta Broughton, Abby Lokszyn, and Debbie Walker. It's for every reader who ever bought one of my books or came to hear me speak. It's also for Betty, Heather, Cindy, Fran, Terri, Alicia, Jack, Bill, Damon, Harry, Al, Jordan, Joe, and everyone who has brought blessings into my life.

About this Book

Quinn Davidson has a knack for choosing the wrong man. She's been with losers, abusers, and just plain jerks. She's tired of the drama, her own and that of her exes. What she wants is a decent, stable man with a good job and a big heart. Too bad she's got a secret that will keep anyone decent a hundred miles away from her.

Tyson Bellamie used to be a football star. Sidelined by an injury, he's fallen back on his education and become principal of the high school in his hometown. Aside from his family, nothing is as important to him as his reputation, which is why when Quinn catches his eye, he's determined to resist her beauty and charm.

Falling in love with Quinn could be the best thing that ever happened to Tyson, but it could ruin his reputation and cost him his job. He just has one choice to make. Will he choose staying with the love of his life, or his all-important career?

Chapter One

Quinn Davidson trudged through the spring drizzle to her car. Work had been crazy today. She was beyond exhausted. She'd been tired and miserable for weeks. It wasn't so much work as it was life in general, keeping her from getting enough sleep. But how could she sleep when her roommate was getting married and moving out?

She was an adult, and quite capable of being alone, but she'd miss Heather. In the few months they'd been roommates, they'd forged a close bond and she'd miss that.

Most days, being a physiotherapist wasn't too physically taxing. But lately, she was working with Tyson Bellamie on rehabbing his knee. He'd blown it out playing pro football and had injured it twice since. As luck, or rather bad luck, would have it, he'd ended up on her patient list. Last year, he'd re-injured his knee by slipping on a wet floor. That injury would have been less severe if he'd done proper rehab after the first accident, the one that ended his career. Same as this current problem. He'd collided with his brother Zander while he and his brothers were playing shinny hockey.

Now, he wanted to be in perfect dancing form for his brother's wedding next month. She had a month to get him in shape and the darn fool refused to set foot in the hospital for rehab. The man was danged lucky the hospital offered in-home services for those willing to pay extra. She wasn't certain why he didn't use a private service, but when her boss said go, she went to patients' homes or offices.

Hot, sweaty, and over-tired, she climbed into her little Kia. Her legs trembled with exhaustion. The frustrating man refused to run on a treadmill, so they ran outside. It wasn't bad when he first started this round of rehab, and they walked outside. She hated running. But if she was going to do the job she was being paid for, she had to run with him to check his stride and watch for potential issues.

"Four weeks left. And then you're done with him," she grumbled and started the little SUV. She rubbed her hands briskly together. Despite jogging, they were cold. She'd forgotten her little gloves. Thankfully, it wasn't that cold, just chilly enough for icy fingers.

She glanced back at Tyson's adorable home as she pulled into the street. Like the chairs in Goldilocks, it wasn't too big or too small, it was just the right size. The green and white bungalow had three bedrooms on the main floor, and one in the walkout basement, near Tyson's workout room. At least that's what he called it. It was more of a full-on weight room. Weights, mirrors, and mats to stretch on. She'd like to get in there alone and play around on the ballet bar which the previous owner had left behind.

She'd started ballet at five and finally quit practicing when she went to college to get her nursing degree. She'd persisted until she had that degree and then gone into physiotherapy. Seven years of education later, she'd moved to Half Moon Bay, and the rest, as they say, was history. She'd been in town five years now and rarely had the opportunity to dance with a man, let alone practice ballet.

As she drove through downtown, she waved at people she knew. Bill Bliss stood outside the Tide's In Café. They'd dated a few times before deciding they weren't compatible and ended up being good friends.

Beth Bellamie, Tyson's mom was chatting away outside Safeway with Ella, her granddaughter. She drove past Bellamie High School, where Tyson was principal. Half the town was named after the Bellamie family. They were one of Half Moon Bay's founding families. She couldn't avoid them, even if she wanted to.

Most of the family were lovely. But Tyson, ugh Tyson. He was stubborn, reserved, and didn't know she was alive. She spent ninety minutes with him three times a week and not once had they had a personal conversation. He treated her like a piece of furniture. He wasn't mean, or rude, just oblivious to the fact that she was a woman. Between that and his refusal to go to the hospital for physio, he pinched her last nerve.

She was pushing thirty-two and starting to want more from her life. Unfortunately, she wanted Tyson. She slapped the steering wheel and pulled into her parking stall behind the red brick apartment building she lived in. She climbed the stairs and opened the door to the suite she shared with Heather Olson. At least they shared for now. Heather would be moving out once she got married to, you guessed it, a Bellamie.

"Heather, I'm home." Her greeting met total silence, and she puffed out a breath. She kicked off her joggers and checked the fridge for notes.

She scanned the short note which read, **Meet me at Take the Cake at seven. Love you, Heather.**

"I guess we aren't carpooling to the cake tasting," she muttered. "Great, now I'm talking to myself. The Bellamies are making me nuts." Okay, Heather wasn't a Bellamie yet, but she was marrying one, so same thing.

A quick shower, something solid to eat before the sweets fest, and she'd be ready. At least she wouldn't have to deal with Tyson tonight. It was Friday, and she was free of him until Monday. She'd call that a blessing.

"You're kidding me, right?" Tyson glared out his kitchen window. "Cake? Do you seriously want me to taste cakes for you? Come on, bro." Tension ratcheted across his shoulders. No way was Zander asking him to do this. His brother knew that he didn't eat sweets.

"Please," Zander begged over the phone. "I just finished a serious surgery and if I don't show up, Heather will be annoyed. This is for her big day, and I don't want to ruin it. I'll owe you."

"Dang right, you will. It's enough that I have to be in the wedding, but cake? I don't eat cake. You know that." After years of living for sport, the eating habits had stuck. He ate a high-protein, low-carb diet. Sweets rarely ever entered the picture. Unless you counted the muffins Zander's fiancée, Heather, made and served at the Half Moon Bay Inn. She made a raisin bran muffin that was to die for. Scrumptious.

"Ty, this is my wedding. You know I'd never ask this of you, but this is an emergency. I just operated on a mama dog with a stuck pup. There's a huge chance of post-surgery complications. I can't just leave them. My assistant is on vacation and the new vet is out sick. Gimme a break. Please."

How could he resist? His extraordinarily talented brother was needed. Saving a life trumped cake every time. "I'll go. But you owe me a pair of Seattle Kraken hockey tickets. Good ones."

"I've got a pair for the Kraken-Canucks game. Third row, center ice. Thanks Ty." He clicked off, obviously in a hurry to return to his patient. Zander's able-bodied receptionist and office assistant Jenny would be on call to pitch in if his brother needed help.

But cake? Seriously? And when he wasn't working out as much as he liked because he'd stupidly injured himself playing shinny with the guys? Bad timing all around.

Twenty minutes later, he stood outside Take the Cake bakery, inhaling the tempting aroma of cinnamon, sugar, and lemon. Cute name for a bakery, but not a place he frequented. As a teenage jock, he'd kicked the sugar habit, but occasionally, he'd give his good knee for a cinnamon roll. He yanked open the door and stomped inside knowing Quinn would be here. As maid of honor, she was helping Heather with everything wedding related. Well, he wouldn't cave into his attraction to her. He was here for cake, and nothing more.

"Hey, Tyson." Yanna greeted him. Her purple hair was caught up in a messy bun.

At twenty-five, she was cute, but totally not his type. She was a great gal, but just too free-spirited. He wanted someone more serious. He had a reputation to uphold as the principal of the high school. Especially if he was going to meet his goal of getting onto the school board.

"Hey, Yanna. I'm here for the cake tasting." He tried not to sound like he was going to a funeral.

"They're in the back." She flashed him a sweet, sexy smile.

"Thanks." He ignored her flirting. "Good to see you." He strode past the register into the back room and stopped dead.

Holy smokes! Quinn had changed from her utilitarian running clothes to a snug wool dress that traced every curve and dip of her enticing figure. He took ten long seconds to memorize the delicious sight. Like a diabetic eying a pretty cake they could never eat, he ogled the woman he could never have.

Of all the rotten luck!

He was about to turn on his heel and bolt when Heather noticed him.

"Tyson! You made it. Zander said you were filling in. It's a good thing you know what your brother likes, or we'd be in a pickle. You're a good man."

"Um. Thanks?"

Heather rushed over and hugged him. "You know Quinn, right?"

"Yes. She's my physiotherapist. Nice to see you both." He tried not to stare at Quinn, at least not any more than he already had.

Her long black hair hung over her shoulders, brushing across the top of her butt. *Man, what a butt.* He jerked his eyes upward. He was not that guy. He never was a womanizer, and he never would be. But holy cow. She had a lovely shape.

Quit it. She's not for you. If he was another man, he'd be more than interested. But she dated. A lot. And that didn't fit in with his plans. Besides, she'd been seeing some jerk for almost a year. Women in committed relationships were off the table.

"Hi, Quinn. Nice to see you. I didn't realize you'd be here." Judging by her glare, she wasn't expecting him either.

He flashed her a cheeky grin which turned into a full-on smirk when her eyebrows snapped together in a frown. He knew it. She was annoyed he was here, but she'd never say anything. Just like she was irked that he chose to run outdoors.

He could go to the hospital for physio, but he hated the smell. Antiseptic, sickness, and dirty socks. It was gag-inducing, despite knowing it was clean. After spending three weeks in a Seattle hospital when he blew his knee, he hated hospitals. He still had nightmares. He'd been told his surgery went well, but on bad nights, his dreams were filled with images of dying on the operating table while they rebuilt his bones and tendons. Besides, he tipped her well for coming to his place.

A tall leggy blonde came into the room and said, "I see we're all here. Let's get this party started." Amanda Brinkley. They'd dated in high school. He'd thought himself in love, but it turned out she was all about him being a football star. When the season ended, she'd ditched him for the captain of the AAA hockey team. So much for true love. Why were women either unsuitable or completely fickle?

"Heather, you and Quinn sit near the wall." She pointed to a table with two chairs on either side. "Tyson, you can sit on this side, near me." She put her hand on his shoulder and urged him forward.

As gently as he could, he shook her hand off. He didn't want her to think, not even for a second, that she had a chance with him.

A twice-divorced woman with five kids? No, thank you. He loved kids but would prefer to raise his own, not someone else's. Though kudos to any man who chose to do so. He slipped out of his jacket and hung it on the back of his chair.

When they were all seated with cups of fresh, hot decaf coffee, she carried a tray of mini cakes over. She cut and served the first and sat beside him, her arm slung over the back of his chair, her hand brushing his shoulder.

He inched forward on his seat. *Nope. Not interested.*

He glanced up and Quinn smirked at him. She raised one eyebrow in question, and he glared back.

"I went a little out of the box with the first cake. You said you wanted something different. This is lemon, with just a hint of thyme."

Tyson eyed the delicious-looking cake suspiciously. Really? He was breaking his no-sweets rule, and she was serving him this? He was half tempted not to taste it at all, except he'd promised Zander. Family could be such a pain in the butt.

He forked up a bit of cake. It was moist and probably amazing ... without the thyme which left a bitter aftertaste on the back of his tongue. He chugged some coffee, nearly scalding his tongue. *Dang it!*

He looked up. Heather tasted the cake without comment. Quinn took the tiniest bite and slipped it into her mouth. Her eyes widened and she made an odd expression that looked suspiciously like a gag. She swallowed twice, sipped her coffee, and said, "Different."

Tyson grinned. She didn't like it. Not one bit. He admired that she was trying to be polite, but the sour expression on her face said she hated it as much as he did.

They sampled three more. All of which were delicious, though he barely ate more than a single, very small, bite.

"What do you think, Tyson?" Heather asked.

He was tempted to say he thought she should bake her own wedding cake, but he bit his tongue. The woman should run a bakery, not a kitchen in an inn. "I think Zander would prefer the carrot cake. It would be my choice from this selection." Plain old chocolate would be his choice, but it wasn't offered.

"I agree," Quinn said with a look that said she hated to agree with him on anything.

They settled on the carrot cake, as well as a nut, egg, and gluten-free choice for their friends who might have special dietary needs.

Quinn was a spitfire for sure. With her quick mind, pretty looks, and great body, she was just the type of woman he was looking for. Except for her dating history

After a few seriously uncomfortable dates, he never dated in town. Instead, he met women from Seattle, Vancouver, or other nearby Canadian and U.S. towns via dating apps and went there to meet them. Rarely did he have more than a second date with any of them. He had high standards. He needed them if he was to maintain his reputation in the community.

Caught up in his thoughts, as he slipped into his coat and turned to go, he almost missed Heather speaking to him.

"Tyson, would you mind running Quinn home? I want to check on Zander. He's probably exhausted."

Great. More time with the woman who had a way of getting under his skin. As if the physio and then cake tasting weren't enough. He sighed. He adored his brother's fiancée like a sister. She was family now and he'd do anything for her. "I can do that. Are you ready Quinn?"

"Two seconds." She gathered up some papers and stuffed them into an accordion folder along with the tablet she'd been making notes on. She probably had a lot to keep track of as maid of honor. Just like he had things to do as best man. For the hundredth time since Zander asked him to fill the position, he wondered why he was chosen over his brothers Derrick and Jacob.

The decision was puzzling, but he loved his brother and was more than happy to be part of the wedding, except for being near Quinn. Something about her made him itchy and unsettled.

"Ready when you are," Quinn said. She hugged Heather. "See you later."

"I might be late." Heather giggled.

Gross. Now he was thinking of Zander and Heather ... He shook the image off. He did not need that mental image in his head. Now or ever. But himself and Quinn ...

Don't go there. She's bad news. Think of your career.

Unfortunately, now that the vision had invaded his brain, and not for the first time, he found it incredibly hard to unsee it.

Chapter Two

Quinn fumed all the way to the truck. *How could Heather do this to her?* Was shoving Quinn and Tyson together a deliberate attempt at matchmaking? Heather didn't like Duke, Quinn's current boyfriend. They'd been off and on for over a year. Heather also knew Quinn was crazy attracted to Tyson.

But really, who wouldn't be? Neatly cut light brown hair. Well-trimmed beard and mustache. Always impeccably dressed. The only time she'd even seen him in a T-shirt was when they were doing physio. He had a respectable job, and a house with a pool and hot tub. He was kind and great with kids. He had strong family ties and was well respected in Half Moon Bay.

She had none of that. Okay, she loved being a physiotherapist. But she had no family unless you counted her estranged cousin in

Hawaii. She lived in a rented apartment which she'd have to give up if she didn't find a roommate soon. She was saving to open her own physio business and if all her money went to rent, she'd never save enough, hence the roommate.

Worst of all, she was beginning to think Heather was right and that Duke was a lost cause. He'd never settle down. He lived in a crappy trailer on the outskirts of town, spent most of his money playing pool and drinking beer. He was always late and when they went out, half the time he forgot his wallet.

Sometimes, he seemed more boy than man. Tyson was all man. Handsome, responsible, caring, and great with his family. Tyson Bellamie was the whole package.

She sighed as she climbed into Tyson's big blue truck. Maybe Heather was right. It was time to ditch Duke. Being single would be better than the grief he put her through. The idea made her sad. She hated being alone. If she dumped him, and Heather moved out, she literally would be alone.

Why were all the good men taken? Or oblivious to her?

"That was a big sigh," Tyson said as he started the truck. He turned to look at her. "Are you okay?"

"Do you ever wish you could scrap your life and start over?" she asked a few blocks later. She snapped her mouth shut. She hadn't meant to confide in him.

"Honestly? Never. I have a few regrets, but I don't need a do-over." He paused. "What's bothering you?"

"Never mind. Please take me home. I appreciate the ride." She had to learn to keep her mouth shut.

"Want to talk about it? We could go for coffee or something. It's early." His mouth snapped shut faster than hers had. He probably regretted asking.

"Are you sure that wouldn't spoil your reputation, Mr. Clean?" She winced; she wasn't usually rude but his inability to see her as a woman was annoying. "Sorry, that was uncalled for."

He pulled over to the curb and parked in front of the Bellamie Curling Rink. "I do worry about my reputation. It is important to me. I don't think that's a bad thing. And no, I'm not worried about being seen with my brother's fiancée's best friend. Now, I repeat, can I buy you a coffee and you can tell me about it?" He paused. "I'm a good listener. At least that's what my students tell me."

She studied him. There was no hint of judgment or concern in his face. He was practically expressionless. Somehow, his calm exterior was reassuring. "Could we get a coffee and go sit somewhere private?" She swallowed her nerves. "Maybe just park in a lot somewhere or something?" Asking for his time felt oddly empowering. Yet it was totally demeaning. *You're a total nut job, Quinn. Totally cray cray.*

"I know just the place."

Fifteen minutes later, two steaming go-cups rested in the cup holders as they traveled past the last streetlight onto the dark highway. It wasn't long before he turned down a road that paralleled the road to his brother Jacob's inn.

"Where are we headed?" she asked. If this were any other man, she'd be nervous. But not only was he a Bellamie, from the most trustworthy family in Half Moon Bay, this was Tyson freaking Bellamie, ex-jock, high school principal, and all-around upstanding citizen. And the hottest man she'd ever met. He had a whole Chris

Hemsworth thing going on. Only better. She was riding through the night with the man of her dreams. Giddy excitement wrapped her like a warm hug.

"There's a place I know. It'll be quiet and it's got a great view. It's just a couple miles." The even tone of his deep voice reassured her. She relaxed into the seat, happy to be spending time with the man she'd fantasized about for years.

He made a left, then a right, and pulled to a stop behind a low row of boulders. The headlights shone out in the darkness. It took a moment to realize they were on a cliff high over the ocean. He shut off the truck and the lights faded to dark. After the bright headlights, the night's blackness was total, soothing, and a bit disconcerting.

He reached behind the seat and grabbed something. "Here's a blanket. Wrap up so we don't need to keep the truck running."

She bundled into the soft, fuzzy throw, and he did the same with a second one. Slowly, one-by-one, stars winked on until the night sky was filled with millions of tiny lights. "I wish I could count all the stars," she whispered.

"There are approximately two hundred billion trillion, that's two hundred sextillion stars, in the universe," he said with all seriousness.

"What? You know that off the top of your head?" She laughed.

"I'm a teacher. I know a lot of things." He sounded totally mocking and smug. Then he laughed. The sound rang loud and deep in the truck and sent a hot shiver straight through her bones.

She reached out and swatted him lightly. "How do you know that?"

"I used to come out here with Dad before he passed. As kids, he used to take us out at night to watch the stars. I know all eighty-eight of the named constellations. Or rather, I did as a kid. I might not remember them all now. It's amazing to look at the sky from other parts of the world." His sigh was almost soundless.

"I've never really traveled. I was born in Seattle. Went to school there. Did a short stint at a hospital in Anchorage during training, and then came here. I'd love to see the world." Something about the total darkness made it easy to share her dreams. She pointed to the sky. "That's Orion's Belt."

"It sure is."

"Look, over there. That's Pegasus." He pointed.

She looked and looked. "I can't see it."

"Lean this way. Follow my finger. It's the box with four 'legs' on the bottom and one out on the top left side of the box, right at the corner."

She moved closer and leaned into him. He was warm and delicious against her shoulder. He smelled of leather and spice. She inhaled the delightful scent and committed the moment to memory. "Where?" she whispered though she could see it clearly now.

He shifted and turned slightly sideways bringing more of his chest into contact with her body. "Look."

She unbuckled and moved closer, leaning her back against his chest. She was cramped by the steering wheel, but it was the best she'd felt in months. She didn't belong in his arms, but it felt too right to move away. She was stealing this moment for her memory box.

"Can you see it?" His breath whispered against her ear, stirring ideas and feelings best left unfelt.

"Oh. There it is." She feigned excitement and reluctantly moved away. If she stayed against him, she'd do something stupid, like kiss him. She would probably never be this close to him again and she was not going to spoil the moment.

She opened her cup and inhaled the sweet scent of hot chocolate. "I love hot cocoa. I think it's my favorite drink."

"I'm more a green tea fan."

"You don't do sweets, do you?" She had often wondered why.

"A holdover from my training days. There was no space for junk food if I was going to stay in peak condition. I watched every bite that went into my mouth. Even now, I don't eat sugar and I rarely drink alcohol. Never soda."

"You're missing out on a lot of great things. Donuts, chocolates, cake—but not lemon and grass cake, or whatever we ate earlier." She groaned.

"That was terrible. I don't know what she was thinking," he chuckled.

"She was thinking she wanted a taste of you." She wanted to call the words back as soon as they left her mouth.

He groaned. "I dated her once. In high school. She dumped me. Now that I'm back, she keeps showing up wherever I am. I'm so tired of women chasing me."

"That must be rough. Poor baby," she teased. What she wouldn't give to have Tyson chasing her. Chasing? Ha! That chase would last eight seconds before she caved to his charms.

"You think I'm playing poor boy, but honestly, a lot of women are more interested in the millions they think I made playing football than they are in me. Frankly, it annoys the heck out of me. Nobody sees me for what I am, just for my supposedly huge bank account."

"And what are you?" She was curious about his opinion of himself.

"I'm exactly what you see. A principal, a brother and son, a quiet stay-at-home type of guy. I'm a man with a solid reputation that I want to keep."

She knew he was all that, but so much more. "And the famous playboy football star with a different girl on his arm every week? What about him?"

"I was never him. Women just showed up where I was. In all the years I played, I only dated twice. Two women, once each. The rest is all just PR crap or flat-out media lies." He scrunched up his face and scraped a hand over his short beard.

His words only made her want him more. She wanted to know everything about him. His favorite foods. His birthday, and his favorite color. Hobbies, passions. Boxers or briefs? "That had to be tough. You seem the quiet type."

"I am," he said, his voice ringing loudly in the quiet night. "I want to find a good woman, settle down, have a few kids, maybe a couple of pets. My dreams are simple." His arm shot out and he grabbed his cup and swilled several mouthfuls. She had the feeling he was trying to shut himself up.

Lord in heaven, his dreams were hers! "I like the future you see. It suits you." A soft sigh slipped out. His plan sounded perfect, but she was stuck in a rut. She needed to get her life together. She needed a man, someone like Tyson, not the boy she was dating.

"We didn't come out here to talk about me. You seemed upset earlier. Want to talk about it?" he asked, his voice barely more than a whisper in the dark.

"Nope."

"Come on, you can trust me. You said you wanted to scrap your life and start over. Do you regret becoming a physio-terrorist?"

"Ha ha." He'd been calling her a physio-terrorist from their first appointment. "No. I love my job. I have some difficult patients who refuse to listen to me," she gave him a pointed look. "But I love my work."

"Is it living in a small town? Do you miss the city?"

"Do you?"

He sighed. "Talking with you is like, I don't know, like trying to push boulders up a hill with a straw. Like Sisyphus, only worse. I'm sure you know his story ... pushing the boulder up the hill forever. Come on, Quinn, talk to me. Mom always says a burden shared is a burden lightened. And for the record, I can't see myself living anywhere but Half Moon Bay. I've turned down a dozen jobs to stay here."

She looked out at the sky through the fog clouding the inside of the windows. "I work long hard hours; at a job I love. I have no family. Only a few friends. My best friend is getting married and moving out. I'm ..." she trailed off.

"You're lonely," he said compassion in his voice He reached out and squeezed her shoulder through the thick throw. "Quinn Davidson, you and I have a lot in common."

She snorted. "Right. You with your mother, three brothers, a niece, friends, coworkers, and women throwing themselves at you. Yup, you're so alone."

"You can be in a crowd and still be lonely," he said with something dark and hurt in his voice.

He was right. "True," she whispered. Her heart clenched. Danged if she didn't like him even more. Coming out here was a mistake.

As if sensing her feelings, he started the truck.

"Are we leaving?"

"Do you want to? I was just going to defog the windows. But if you'd like to leave, we can go."

The question ricocheted in her mind. Stay or go? Go or stay? "I think, if you don't mind, I'd like to stay a bit longer." She'd take every second that he'd give her. She'd squirrel them away to revisit later. When he'd moved on with his life and got back to not knowing she existed.

"Done."

They sat in comfortable silence for a long time. She was almost drifting off when he cried out. "Look a shooting star!"

She looked up but it was too late. "I missed it."

"Maybe we'll see another. They often come in groups."

Sure enough, a few minutes later a bright streak shot across the sky, low, near the horizon. "Look," she exclaimed. "Make a wish." She closed her eyes and wished for the one thing that her heart truly wanted. Tyson Bellamie.

Chapter Three

O ne thing Tyson knew for certain. He was glad it was Saturday. It was an unusual weekend for him. He didn't have any work to catch up on. He'd spent a good part of his Christmas break catching up. Some days, it seemed like his work was never done. Today, aside from his exhaustion at staying up too late with Quinn, and then tossing and turning half the night, he was as free as a bird.

He lay in bed considering what to do today. He'd visit his mother. Maybe take her out for lunch if she didn't already have plans. He'd swing by the inn and see Jacob, Lexi, and Ella. He adored his niece. For a teenager, she was pretty cool.

He wondered what Quinn's plans for the day were. He knew she had weekends off because he'd tried to book appointments on the weekend, and it was rarely possible. She should open her own therapy business. She'd make a killing. He'd worked with dozens of therapists and trainers over the years, and she was, by far, the most talented. It was why he insisted on her for his rehab. A generous donation to the hospital had ensured she was assigned to him. He almost felt guilty about using his money to get his way, but in a place as small as Half Moon Bay, the hospital always needed extra funds.

During physio, Quinn knew when to push and when to back off. She had a gift for saying the right thing to wring one more rep out of him. And her warning look would quell a bigger man than he was.

He'd been surprised to hear she was upset with her life. She was always upbeat and seemed to have her life together. Except for the guy she dated. Why was a wonderful woman like her hooked up with a nothing like Duke? It didn't make sense.

His phone beeped with a text message.

Mom: Meet me at Anchors Aweigh at 10:45 for brunch?

Ty: Sure. Want a ride?

Mom: I'll walk. It's barely below freezing.

Ty: K.

Mom: Would it kill you to type the entire word? It's only four letters.

Ty: It might. :)

He hopped out of bed when he realized that it was already ten o'clock. He'd slept much later than normal. He'd need to take a fast shower. Of course, he'd been awake until three because something about Quinn Davidson was stuck in his head.

The hot water and soapy smell revived him. He did love a good shower. He wondered if Quinn was a bath or shower girl. Personally, he loved his hot tub but hated lying in a regular bathtub. What did her preferences matter? Quinn wasn't the woman for him. He needed stability.

Okay, she wasn't unstable exactly, but she had a bit of a reputation for dating a lot.

He sighed. She'd been with Duke a long time. He tried to figure out how long, but they didn't exactly run in the same circles. He just knew it was at least a year. Thinking about Quinn and Duke, or any other man, scraped against Ty's nerves. She deserved better.

He soaped and scrubbed and tried to plan his day, but thoughts of Quinn kept intruding. When the water ran cold, he rinsed off the last of the soap and got out.

His coffee maker was programmed to make a pot at seven every morning. The once delicious coffee had become sludge from sitting for so long, but he needed the jolt of caffeine to kick Quinn out of his head. He poured himself a cup and added a healthy slug of milk to offset the burnt taste. Why was it, he mused, did old coffee smell like an ashtray?

He strode into Anchors Aweigh and was instantly taken back to another time. The bar was a great place to eat but the décor was old tavern meets the nineteen-seventies. The burnished wood-topped bar was beautiful, but in his opinion, the macramé plant hangers and fake coconut decorations were dated and just a bit tacky, as were the sunken ship decorations. The lantern-style lights would be okay if the rest were updated to be less cheesy. Maybe the cheesy décor appealed to tourists. Half Moon Bay was a tourist town after all.

The best thing about Anchors Aweigh was the food. Every item on the menu was delicious. Brad, the owner and chef had mad kitchen skills. He'd grown up in the restaurant and bought it from his parents a couple years earlier. His sister Sammi was dating Tyson's brother Derrick.

He paused in the doorway letting his eyes adjust to the dim interior. Outside was brilliantly sunny. Inside, while not dark, felt like a dungeon in comparison. He peered around the busy room. His mother stood near the back, frantically waving at him. She wasn't alone.

Crap!

He cast a quick prayer upwards that she wasn't trying to set him up. Again. She'd pushed Jacob and Lexi together. And Zander and Heather. And Sammi and Derrick. With all his brothers in happy, healthy relationships, he'd known he was next.

Bracing for disaster he strode through the room, swerving between tables, and greeting teachers, parents of his students, and friends as he passed. Halfway across the room, his eyes adjusted fully, and he realized that his mom sat next to Heather, and if he was any judge, that long black hair on the person with her back to him was Quinn.

Setup? Coincidence? He was leaning toward the latter. One never knew with his mom.

"Morning, ladies." He bussed his mom on the cheek and smiled at Heather. Manners dictated that he acknowledge Quinn as well. "Morning, Quinn." He sat beside her. The sweet scent of strawberries washed over him.

Her face turned delightfully pink as he sat beside her. Odd.

She cleared her throat. "Hi, Tyson."

His mother glanced at her watch. "You're late," she chided gently.

"I was busy."

"Doing what? Your hair is still wet." She gave him 'the look'. "Tyson Bellamie, you were still in bed when I texted. Weren't you?"

He laughed. He never could pull one over on his mother. "Yes, I was. I was up late last night and decided to sleep in." He gave a brief nod to acknowledge her win.

"Oh? Hot date?"

"I don't know that I'd call it a date, but I was having coffee with a friend."

Quinn choked slightly on her coffee.

"A female friend?" his mother, Beth, asked gleefully.

Oh, dear Lord. How did he extract himself from this one? If he said there was no chance of dating, Quinn could be hurt. If he said there was, she might get her hopes up for nothing. He snorted internally. As if she was interested in him. They'd known each other for years, and unlike a lot of women, she'd never made a play for him.

"Mom, I don't need you finding me dates. I'm only thirty-three. There's no rush to get married."

"Well, as you get older, the women you date will get older. If you plan on having kids, you better get to it. Women can only have kids for so long before it becomes a health risk."

Heat crept up his face and both Quinn and Heather stared at his mom with wide, startled eyes.

"How about we table this discussion for later?" he asked.

"Fine." His mother crossed her arms and glared. "But I think it's time for you to grow up and get married. Quinn is a lovely young lady. Maybe you two should go out. You might hit it off." She smiled like she'd just delivered a 'Mom of the Year' speech.

Quinn went beet red. Heather laughed.

"Yes, she is. But I'm not dating right now."

"Oh, I know." Beth snapped her fingers. "You can get to know each other at Heather and Zander's wedding. It's only a month away. You'll walk out of the church together. You'll sit side by side at the head table. Oh, you'll dance together," she added excitedly.

"Mom! Stop!" He kept his voice low, but firm. "I. Am. Not. Dating."

She crossed her arms and looked hurt. "Fine. But don't blame me when you die a lonely old bachelor."

He hated hurting her, but she'd gone too far. He sipped the water which was sitting at his place when he arrived and looked at her. Was that a smirk? She was totally trying to pull a fast one. He was half tempted to call her on it.

A server stepped up to the table. "Are you folks ready to order?"

His mom ordered the senior's bacon and eggs. Quinn and Heather both ordered burgers and salads. After quick consideration, he ordered an egg white omelet with peppers, onions, and mushrooms, with a side of turkey bacon.

"At least have real bacon," his mother said.

"Fine. Make that real bacon, please."

Once the server walked away, an uncomfortable silence fell over the table. Around them, the clatter of silverware and happy chatter filled the spaces between classic rock music, notably Jimmy Buffet. Tyson floundered for a way to fill the conversational gap without bringing up marriage or dating.

"What are you ladies up to today?" he asked.

"We're meeting Lexi and Ella for my final dress fitting," Heather exclaimed. "I'm so excited to see how it fits after the alterations. The bridesmaids are all getting their dresses too. Zander said you guys are already prepped with tuxes. You should see the bridesmaids' dresses. They're beautiful. Quinn's going to look so hot!" Excitement for her upcoming nuptials rang in every word. Why did women get so excited about weddings?

"The dresses are pretty," Quinn blurted. "Everyone will look very nice." Her cheeks went even pinker than earlier. The poor girl was going to combust.

"I'm sure you'll all look lovely." He smiled. "Even now, you are positively glowing Heather. What's Zander up to today?"

"Oh, he's working." She mock pouted. "He's been watching his patient from yesterday. Poor thing is still in a bad place. Luckily the pup has the best veterinarian in the United States looking after him."

She wasn't just boasting. Zander had saved some animals a lot of vets would have given up on. Last year he'd saved a pregnant fox who had been hit by a car. Several months later, the fox and her kits had been released into the wild.

"Maybe I'll swing by and visit him."

"He'd love that," Heather said.

Conversation turned to mundane things, and he breathed a sigh of relief. He was so tired of women hitting on him and of people trying to set him up. First thing he would do when he got home was find someone on one of his dating apps. He'd set up a couple of dates for next weekend. Preferably in Seattle.

His mom was right. He should be married. He wanted to be married. But he was going to do the choosing. He'd find someone in another town and move them home. It was a simple matter of creating a plan and executing it.

Honestly, it wasn't much different than football. You created a play, put things in motion, and followed them through. Before long, he'd score the perfect wife. One who would support his career and reputation. One he could love and who would love him, and their children with all their hearts. He just wanted to find her himself.

Chapter Four

Lunch was interminable. She'd joined Heather and Beth thinking it would be a girl's morning. No such luck. She was stunned when Tyson arrived and sat beside her. All through the meal their elbows and knees bumped. Each brush sent warmth rushing through her until she thought she'd combust. Now she understood when her mother had complained about hot flashes. Yikes!

It was all she could do to eat her burger. She barely touched her fries. She was so nervous sitting beside Tyson. He radiated a sweet heat she wanted to snuggle into. She was both relieved and disappointed when breakfast ended. By the time they left, she was a quivering bundle of nerves and her thighs ached from holding herself in place. She'd leaned against him last night, and no matter how much she wanted to be near him, she was not going to cave to that temptation again. She was stronger than that.

Twenty minutes into the dress fittings, she was still twitchy with nerves. She sat in the corner of the ultra-feminine dress shop while Heather tried on her gown. Satin and Bows was known statewide for their amazing custom dresses as well as their wide selection of off-the-rack ladies' wear.

Her thoughts flowed to the bridesmaids' dresses and then to the men's tuxes. Oh, sweet heaven. How was she going to survive Tyson in a tux? In a suit he was devastating, in shorts for his training sessions, he was enough to make her lose all her professionalism. But a tux? She'd never keep her hands off him.

"Quinn?"

A sharp elbow slammed into her ribs. She glared at Lexi. "What?"

"It's your turn to try on your dress," Heather said. "Where were you? You must have been miles away. Were you thinking about a guy?" she teased. Quinn heartily wished her roommate didn't know who she'd spent the evening with last night. She was going to get all sorts of unrealistic ideas about Quinn joining the Bellamie clan.

"Ha. As if. The only guy in my life is Duke."

"Ew," Lexi groaned. "I've only met him once, but yuck." She paled then turned bright pink. "Oh. I'm sorry. I didn't mean to dis your man. He's, um, he's just not my type."

"He better not be," Beth teased, "You're with my son now."

"I was just wool-gathering. I was up late last night and I'm a bit woolly-headed today." She jumped up. "Let me at that dress." She wanted to die of mortification for being caught dreaming about a guy she would never and could never have.

"Duke's not so bad," she defended the man she'd been dating. He wasn't terrible, but he wasn't great either. But he kept her from being alone. She had yet to invite him to be her plus one at the wedding and a tiny part of her felt guilty about that.

The attendant led her to a dressing room where her beautiful emerald green dress hung on the wall. "I'll let you put it on," the woman said. "I'll be right outside if you need me." She pulled the door shut with a soft click.

Quinn stripped and slid into the deep green silk dress. It floated around her like a cloud. Off the shoulder cap sleeves accentuated her neck and the shape of her arms. It was a good thing she worked out or her arms would look like sausages. The neckline had the slightest dip in the center and the hem swirled just above her knees. It was totally modest, and at the same time very sexy. She stepped out of the dressing room and strode to the pedestal before a set of triple mirrors.

She stepped up and examined herself from all angles. Even in sock feet, the dress was amazing.

"You look incredible. You're going to slay all the single men," Heather exclaimed. "Let's see us all together."

Quinn realized that everyone else was already in their dress, even Ella. The dresses were all the same shade of green, but each style was chosen to suit its wearer's body and personality. They stood side by side looking into the mirrors. Every one of them wore a beautiful smile.

"We look dang good," Quinn declared. "We're going to knock 'em dead at the wedding." She turned to hug Heather. "Thank you for having me in your wedding, and for choosing such beautiful dresses."

"I second that," Beth declared. As mother of the groom, her dress was a different style and shade of green, but it was accented with the same lovely green as the bridesmaids' dresses. She stepped back from the others and held up her hands to encompass them all. "Look at all my girls. You are so beautiful. You make my heart full."

Quinn tried to smile back, but her heart wasn't in it. She wasn't part of the Bellamie family, no matter how much she wished she was. Her body turned cold, as unhappiness washed over her. She pasted on a fake smile and slipped away to change out of her dress. She needed a moment to steady herself.

Once this wedding was over, she'd be free of Tyson Bellamie's lure. She'd never have to see him again. By that time, his physio would be complete and there would be no more runs with him.

She laughed out loud as she undid her dress's side zipper. Right! Because she'd never see him around town, or if she visited Heather and Zander. She sighed in disappointment at the thought, even as her heart jumped at the idea of seeing him again. Maybe this was just a case of wanting what she couldn't have.

As she pulled on her jeans, she contemplated her dating life. It wasn't satisfactory as it was, that's for sure. She'd ditch Duke as soon as she worked up the courage. Then, she'd sign up for one of those dating apps and go fishing. There were good men out there and it was high time she started searching.

A smile blossomed as she slid into her sweater. Having a plan to move forward with felt a-maz-ing. Giddy warmth filled her heart and she found herself whistling as she returned the dress to its hangar.

"Are you seeing Duke tonight?" Heather asked as they climbed the stairs to their apartment.

So much for her good mood. She frowned. "No. He's out of town. Visiting his folks or something. It's a quiet night in for me. What about you?" She pulled her keys out of her pocket and unlocked the door.

"Dinner at Beth's. It's funny how one can get used to their brand of love. Such chaos." She laughed. "Everyone pokes and prods and tries to get a reaction out of everyone else. It's like a good-natured brawl. Zander's always the peacekeeper. Beth's always exasperated. Derrick's calmed down since realizing he loves Sammi but he still tends to be a grump. It's an absolute zoo and I love it." She hung up her jacket and whirled to face Quinn. "You totally should come. I know Beth would love to have you."

"I could never intrude on a family dinner." But Lord, how she wanted to. "I've got an H.M. Shander romance and some hot cocoa waiting for me."

"Well, if you change your mind, text me. I'm spending the afternoon keeping Zander company before dinner. I'm leaving as soon as I check my email. I'm waiting for confirmation on the price of my wedding flowers."

Quinn finished her deliciously steamy book and did a bit of yoga. She was stiff from running with Tyson. Danged stubborn man and his refusal to run on a treadmill even though he owned one. He was as frustrating as he was attractive.

Enough thoughts of Tyson.

She pushed him aside and started another book. Thank heaven for e-readers and library cards. She was never without a good book. Supper was a tasteless frozen pizza and three glasses of wine.

"You shouldn't drink alone," she chided herself as she poured a fourth glass. "Why not? It's not like I'm an alcoholic. I drink maybe once a month." She argued with herself for a moment and decided that this was her last glass. Maybe it would be enough to make her mind stop imagining Tyson as the hero in every scene in her book. The man was like a barnacle she couldn't scrape off.

She was barely seated when someone pounded on her door. The building had a buzzer system. She was going to have to complain about people letting strangers into the building. She ignored the knocking. She wasn't expecting anyone. The thumping persisted. She set her reader aside, rose, and looked out the peephole.

Duke.

Oh, for Pete's sake.

She sighed and unlocked the door. She opened it a crack and said, "Duke. I thought you were out of town."

He flung his arms wide. "I'm back, doll-face." He pushed his way inside. He reeked of beer. Apparently, he'd been back for a while. "I came to see you for my birthday kiss."

Shoot. She'd forgotten it was his birthday. "Happy birthday." She shut the door and followed him to the couch.

"Don't I get a birthday kiss?" He grinned leaning forward.

She woke up in the morning, head pounding. She rolled over with a groan and bumped right into Duke's chest.

Crap!

She'd been going to dump him. He'd insisted on a birthday drink. She'd gotten him a drink and sipped her wine, preparing to dump him. Realization hit her like a brick wall. She must have been drunker than she realized.

She smacked him on the shoulder. "Duke, get up." Time to do the right thing, get rid of him, and start treating herself better.

He grumbled and rolled over. "What's up, babe?"

"You're up. Up and out of my house. We're done. Through. I don't ever want to see you again."

"But, babe," he whined. "We're so good together. We make magic in the sheets." He stroked her arm.

She slapped his hand away. "You know what? We're not good in the sheets. Frankly, you're terrible. I'm done with you. Out," she stabbed a finger toward the door. She grabbed a blanket and wrapped herself up. "I don't ever want to see you again." She trembled with anger. What kind of a man had sex with a drunk woman?

Cussing and grumbling, he stumbled into his clothes. "I'll be back for my stuff."

"What stuff? You never left so much as a toothbrush here." How had she thought they were in a serious relationship. She rarely saw his friends, didn't know his family, and they never went out.

He was using me all along and I was too stupid to notice it.

"Don't come back. Ever. If you do, I'll have you arrested for stalking."

"You are such a witch. I'm glad to be done with you!" He slammed the door on the way out.

She stared at the door for several seconds before locking it. She waited for the sadness to hit, for the loneliness to swamp her. Nothing. She grinned. She wasn't upset. She was elated. She let out a loud whoop and giggled. She should have done that months ago.

Whistling happily, she stripped the bed and tossed the sheets into the laundry. While she waited for them to wash, she scrubbed up the slushy mud he'd left all over the floor by the door. The man couldn't even put his boots on the mat.

She fired up the stereo and danced herself silly, blending random dance with ballet moves. This was the best day ever. She was free! She felt like a new woman. Suddenly starving, she decided to make muffins and went to the kitchen.

Heather had left a note on the fridge that she'd been home and was spending the day with Zander. *No surprise there.* But she would be home in time to cook supper.

Perfect!

They'd have a fabulous girl's night in and celebrate her newfound single status.

Chapter Five

C areer day was one of Tyson's favorite days of the year. He loved watching his students interact with adults in different occupations. Back in his youth, everyone sat in the gymnasium and listened to boring talk after talk. He'd changed that up when he took over the school. Now, adults with different careers sat at tables around the gym and two classes at a time, students came in and walked around talking to anyone who interested them.

He had reps from four colleges and universities with tables to cover the basics. He had three trade schools as well as reps from a variety of fields. Engineering, chemistry, nursing. A chef, a lawyer, a concert pianist, a local musician, and Zander was there to talk about being a vet. To his surprise and chagrin, Quinn showed up in place of the physiotherapist he was expecting.

As he did with all his guests, Tyson greeted Quinn with a warm welcome and a handshake. Electricity shot up his arm. Her eyes went wide. She must have felt it too. He dropped her hand like a hot potato before she seared her brand onto him. "Ms. Davidson, welcome."

"Thanks. But please call me Quinn. I find a casual feel helps appointments go more smoothly. Your students can call me Quinn as well. I can't disclose names, but several of your students are my patients."

"Quinn it is. I was expecting Jill Brown."

"Jill has a bit of a stomach bug. She's out for a day or two. Fortunately, our patient load is light this week. I was able to shuffle patients around to be here."

"Bellamie High School appreciates that." He suppressed a wince at his formality.

She smiled. "Happy to serve." She saluted him. "Where do you want me?"

A totally unacceptable answer sprung to his lips. He swallowed the inappropriate response and consulted his tablet. "You're on the far wall, second table from the end." He pointed. "Right there beside the bakery."

"Oh good. Maybe they'll have snacks. My stomach is jumpy this morning. Maybe a bite would settle it."

"I hope you aren't getting the flu. I can find you a snack from the staff room if you'd like." He was surprisingly eager to please her.

"I doubt it's the flu. I skipped breakfast to fit in a patient. I'll be fine," she squeezed his arm reassuringly. "Now, I'll just set up my stuff." She pointed to a rolling bin at her feet. "I brought some of the tools of the trade as well as brochures from the school I attended. I hope that's okay."

"It's perfect. I check in on you later." Reluctantly, he turned his attention to Officer Singe who stood behind Quinn. Though he was talking to the police officer, half his attention was on watching Quinn walk away. She was wearing her loose-fitting hospital scrubs. But his gaze kept sneaking to her backside. Not good. *Rein it in! She's not for you and you're working.* He'd be mortified if any of his students or staff caught him leering at a woman.

Part of him couldn't help but wonder what it would be like to be in a relationship with an upbeat and happy person like Quinn. Aside from physio where she was all business, one lunch, and one short evening of frankly serious discussion, he'd barely spent any time with her. But it was enough to know she was intelligent, quick-witted, and upbeat. After the last four dates he'd been on, he was beginning to realize personalities like Quinn's were rare.

He suppressed a shudder thinking about his last dates. One woman morphed from a pretty blonde picture to a tattooed goth. The brunette turned out to be a raving political fanatic. He respected everyone's political opinions, but to suggest that certain humans should be culled was too extreme. Neither of the other two could stop ranting about their exes. Frankly, the dating pool was starting to depress him.

He wandered from table to table, silently watching interactions between guests and grade eleven students. Several students earned a quelling glare for goofing off, but for the most part, everyone was well-behaved and engaging in meaningful conversations.

He listened to Marcy from the bakery explain that she wasn't there to hire people, but if the young man would stop by the bakery with an application, she would look it over. He moved on to watch Quinn interact with a group of girls.

"Honestly," she said looking from girl to girl, "physiotherapy can be hard. You have to deal with uncooperative patients, with patients who might never heal, or with over-eager ones who push too hard and re-injure themselves. But the rewards are completely worth it. You get to help people learn to walk again or show them how to cope with new disabilities. You meet a wide variety of people from all walks of life. I've met several lifetime friends through my work."

"What courses do I need to take physio?"

"I'd recommend a strong base in the sciences, English, and math. Being able to spell difficult words is huge during charting, and especially while studying. You'll come across anatomy and physiology words that will trip you up repeatedly. A sound grounding in English will help. A lot. Trust me. I had to take remedial English, on my own time, to build the foundation I was lacking."

"I'm a great speller. I never need spell check," one girl exclaimed.

"I love science," the other said.

"Sounds like you'd be a great study team," Quinn encouraged. "You'll be able to help each other out. My recommendation is that you look around today. Talk to everyone, even about careers you've never considered. You never know what's going to catch your interest. I wanted to be a paleontologist until I discovered physiotherapy as a possibility in university."

"We'll do that." The girls wandered away.

Once they were out of earshot, Quinn looked at him and said, "Did I do okay? I wasn't expecting so many questions."

"That was incredible. Just what they need to hear without gloss, but still encouraging. You're good with kids."

"Well, I do work with them all the time," she said wryly. "And I intend to have a few of my own someday."

"You and me both."

"What? Five hundred students aren't enough for you?" Her grin said she was teasing.

"Some days, they are more than enough. But generally, no. I love children and am hoping to have my own."

Her understanding smile warmed something in him and made him wonder how a woman he'd known professionally for years, and more recently casually, had escaped his notice for so long. Okay, he had noticed her, but she wasn't his type.

"Do you plan to work after you have children?"

"Do you," she quipped, arms crossed over her chest.

"Touché. Stupid question. Or rather, a poorly worded question. What I meant was have you considered how family life will affect your career? I know I've put a lot of thought into it."

"I have, though I'm not sure this is an appropriate venue for this discussion," she said quietly. Her gaze danced around the room.

He looked around. Several sets of eyes and ears were turned in their direction.

"Perhaps we could have coffee and talk about it?"

The suggestion was half question. He warmed at the thought, even as a chill went through him. As appealing as Quinn was, she wasn't for him.

"Perhaps." He tried to smile. "Thanks for coming out today Ms. Davidson. Bellamie High School appreciates your presence." He nodded briskly and walked to the next table. He could almost feel her eyes on him as he talked to the plumber next to her.

He risked a glance her way. Yup, she was staring at him, a puzzled look in her eyes. He may have just opened a can of worms.

Chapter Six

Quinn knocked on Tyson's front door on Saturday. She was fifteen minutes late. Over the past two days, ever since eating at a seafood truck on the beach with a coworker on Thursday night, she'd been plagued by stomach upset. This morning was the worst. Her butt was dragging. She was exhausted and queasy. From here on out, she'd stick to places she knew and curb her desire to try new eating establishments.

Tyson opened the door. "You're late." His smile went straight to her heart. How many years had she been dreaming of being the recipient of that smile? Too dang many, that's for sure.

"Sorry, I'm fighting the lingering effects of food poisoning." She rubbed her mittened hands briskly together. Spring was fast approaching, but it was still cold on the hands. This close to the ocean, the humidity seemed to exacerbate the cold. "But I'm good to go."

His brow wrinkled and his bright smile faded. "Are you sure? I could use the treadmill."

"Naw. I'm good." She'd gotten used to their thrice weekly runs and the time spent with him. While she wasn't a fan of jogging, she'd rather be running and distracted, than sitting and watching all those muscles flex as he went through the paces on the treadmill. The man had amazing legs, despite the large surgery scars. Besides, she'd firmed up and dropped a few pounds since she added running to her routine.

"Promise to tell me when you've had enough?"

"Tyson Bellamie, are you trying to get out of running?" She shook her finger at him but couldn't stop her smile. "When have I ever let you skimp on your physio?"

"Never. You're a tyrant." His carefree laugh startled her. She's seen him like this with his family, but never with her. Their relationship was strictly professional.

"Being a tyrant is my job. Now lock up, or I'm going home for a nap." He keyed in his code and the deadbolt slid shut with a hiss and click. She gestured ahead of her. "You first, I want to watch your gait."

"Are you sure you aren't watching my backside?"

Heat flooded her face. Okay, maybe she was. A little. Not that she'd ever give him the satisfaction of admitting it. He stopped so abruptly that she almost slammed into him. "Get moving," she demanded in her best no-nonsense voice.

He winked and took off at a slow jog.

"Walk," she shouted. He knew the routine. A walk to assess gait, then more evaluation as they eased into a slow jog. Only when she was satisfied, he was still moving without issue, did they run. When she was certain he was moving without a limp or poor posture, she caught up to him and ran by his side. They'd slowly built up from a hundred yards to three miles.

Yesterday's skiff of snow had melted off the sidewalks, though there were a few icy spots to watch for. It was pretty with the grass still snowy and the streets wet. The early morning was quiet and peaceful. Traffic was almost nonexistent as the sun rose slowly in the clear sky.

Within a couple of blocks, her breathing came in painful gasps. That food poisoning had really taken it out of her. She was as weak as a newborn kitten.

"You're dragging," he said, slowing down slightly. "Are you sure you're okay?"

She glanced over at him. "I'm fine."

"You're pale too. Are you sick?"

"Maybe not quite recovered from that food poisoning," she admitted. "I've got this. Keep going."

He nodded. At the next corner he made a right turn, and again at the next corner. He was headed for home. She grabbed his arm and yanked him to a stop. "Keep going. We aren't done yet."

"We might not be done yet, but you are. I'll finish on the treadmill while you watch. I'm the one who needs physio, not you. Besides, we only have a few sessions left."

"You're scheduled for three more weeks. That's nine sessions." She ground the words out between gasps. She hated to admit that he was right to turn back.

"I think I'm probably good to quit training with you now."

She swallowed her disappointment. Technically, he was probably fine. He wasn't taking part in sports these days. He kept fit working out in his home gym. If he was still a pro athlete, she'd recommend more training. The truth was she didn't want to stop working with Tyson. This was the only way she got to be in his company. Dang her traitorous heart.

"That's up to you," she said at last as he slowed to a walk.

"It is," he agreed. "You don't agree?"

"Professionally, I think at least a few more sessions are in order." She paused to formulate her words. "If you're thinking of playing hockey, football, or any other active sport, I highly recommend we keep training."

"The only sport on my horizon is dancing at Zander and Heather's wedding."

She wondered about his real reason for stopping training. She knew what he made as a pro-football player and could guess at what he earned as a high school principal. Heather had mentioned that each of the Bellamie brothers had received a lump sum inheritance when their father died. So, it wasn't a money issue.

"Is it the time of day we work out?" She pressed her hand into the cramp in her left side, just under her ribs.

"Nope. I just think I'm done. I know my body and my knee is as good as it is going to get. I'll keep up my routine. I swear."

He almost sounded like he was asking for her permission. "That's a good plan, you don't want to risk injury. Honestly, I recommend we keep working together. But in the end, it is up to you. Maybe you'd like a different trainer."

"Nope." He paused at an intersection to let a car pass and waved at the occupants.

"There are three physio therapists at the hospital. You could probably take your pick." She crossed her fingers that he wouldn't change his trainer.

"I paid for you because I wanted you. I worked with the others. I don't find them as motivating as I find you."

"And you're giving me the boot?" Professionally, she understood that he was well within his rights to change their treatment plans. Personally, she didn't want to lose one second of time with him.

"Nothing personal," he said as they climbed the steps to his front door. "I'm just done."

"I'll cancel your appointments." She followed him inside.

"I'm going to have some OJ before I finish my run. Do you want anything?"

"No, I'm good. I'll just use the washroom." The thought of orange juice made her stomach clench. She kicked off her shoes and hurried toward the bathroom. She barely made it inside before she brought up the tea and toast she'd had for breakfast.

She tried to be quiet. No sense in letting Tyson know she was ill. She'd be fine in a minute. She rinsed her mouth and sat on the edge of the tub to catch her breath. What in the world? She'd been fine most of yesterday. What kind of stomach flu came in waves?

"Are you okay in there?" he called through the door.

"Yup." Her voice shook and she swallowed hard. "I'm fine."

He muttered something and walked away.

Feeling slightly better, she rinsed again, used the mouthwash she found on the counter, and made her way to the kitchen. The rising sun shone through the windows highlighting the light oak cabinets and their golden knobs. A bouquet of fresh daisies sat on the table, close to the wall. She'd never been in this room before. They usually went straight to the basement. She liked his stainless-steel appliances, and the adorable football shaped cookie jar, though she doubted he used it for cookies. Two matching towels hung precisely on the oven door and the sink and counter were clear of dishes. He was a neat housekeeper.

"I made you some mint tea." He set it on the table. "Take a minute to soothe your stomach."

"Thanks."

He opened a cupboard and pulled out a box of saltines and removed a clip from the end of an open stack. He put them on the table. "Mom says crackers help with stomach upset."

She nibbled a cracker and began to feel better. "Let's take this downstairs. I can have tea while you run. Then we can get into the strength training."

She followed him downstairs, stomach protesting with every step. With luck she'd feel better tomorrow. She couldn't afford to be off work. Not and stay on track to open her own business.

Chapter Seven

Tyson propped his feet up on the railing of Zander's deck. His brother had a deck heater running and they sat under its warmth staring out at the Friday evening sky.

"What's wrong with you these days?" Zander demanded.

Tyson glared at his brother. "Not a danged thing. I'm just busy at work."

"Since when is that a factor? You're always busy. You need to learn to delegate more. None of your staff works the stupid long hours you do." He sipped his beer like he hadn't just been offensive.

"Would you listen to Mister Lives at Work?" Tyson was grumpy and he'd be hanged if he could figure out why. Aside from the fact that he wasn't sleeping well, life was good. His physio was finished so he had more free time, though he spent a lot of it in the office or driving to out-of-town dates.

He'd gotten in the habit of booking three or four dates a weekend. Lunch and dinner on both Saturday and Sunday. So far, he'd flat-out struck out. None of his dates measured up to the one woman he'd never have.

Quinn popped into his head at the strangest moments, totally distracting him from whoever his current date was. He tried to push aside his dating woes and focus on his family. Because all else aside, he was looking forward to watching Zander get married.

Okay, maybe there was a bit of jealousy because he was the last brother to find a life mate. He always thought he'd be first, and here he was dead last with no prospects in sight.

"I need a favor," Zander abruptly changed the subject.

"Sure." Anything to distract himself from thoughts of Quinn.

"I need you to drive into the city tomorrow and pick up some stuff. Heather has a list, and neither of us can get away."

"Can't you order online? Or pick it up in town?"

"I wish. We've tried. Half Moon Bay is a wonderful place to live, but the shopping can be less than ideal. You're always in the city. What's one more trip?

After a moment of thought to consider his schedule for the weekend, he said, "I suppose you're right. I'll have to reschedule a date, but that's no problem." He'd been debating canceling anyway. He was tired of putting on a bright face for the endless stream of women. Besides, his wallet was taking a hit, and he wasn't made of money. But for his brother's happiness, he'd gladly make the long drive again.

"Give me a list and I'm on it. What do you need?"

"Heather has the list. There are orders waiting at several suppliers and a couple decisions to make as well. Can you take Quinn? She knows what Heather has in mind." He threw the question out casually, but Tyson suspected there was more to it.

"Why bother her when I can probably do it alone?" He didn't need more Quinn in his life. He needed someone like Quinn, but not the actual Quinn.

"Heather wants Quinn to pick out some table linens, or something. I don't know. I just want this wedding over and done with so I can start my married life. Heather and I belong together. If she wants Quinn to do this, I'm fine with it. Happy spouse, happy house." He grinned and toasted his absent fiancée with his beer.

Tyson didn't respond. If he said anything about avoiding Quinn, Zander would ride him for weeks, which was the last thing he needed.

"Is going with Quinn a problem for you?" He arched a brow.

In the silence that followed, a coyote howled, followed by the yip of pups and the hoot of an owl. Tyson loved the natural silence of Zander's rural home.

"Well, is being with Quinn going to be a problem?" Zander pushed.

"Nope. Quinn's a nice woman."

"Ever thought about dating her?"

"Nope. She's not my type."

"What? How can a beautiful, compassionate, smart, and gainfully employed woman not be your type? Dude, are you gay? I mean you never date."

"I date, just not in Half Moon Bay. I have a reputation to protect. Being a serial dater would trash that."

"Are you a serial dater?" Zander always knew how to throw an accurate verbal punch and this one hit right on the mark.

He sighed. "Probably." He stood and wandered restlessly up and down the second story deck. "I'm looking for someone I can connect with. Someone who shares my values and life goals. Someone who won't ruin my reputation." God, he sounded selfish when he spoke his needs aloud.

"I get it."

"How could you possibly understand? You were hell-bent on bachelorhood until Heather stumbled into your path." Heather, a chef at their brother's inn, had showed up at Zander's vet clinic with a 'wild' animal in the car. She'd been freaked out. As it turned out, the animal was only a domestic cat seeking shelter from the rain. The cat was now a shop pet, along with Zander's dog. Heather had nearly gotten over her absolute terror of animals and loved both critters.

"Yup." He grinned. "She showed me what I was missing." He sipped his beer. "I was dating outside of town too. "Not because I was looking for anything permanent, and not just a hookup. I was looking for simple companionship and you know as well as I do that as soon as Mom sees us with a woman, she starts hearing wedding bells." He laughed wryly.

"That's the hard truth," Tyson agreed.

"Bro, you're missing out. Family is everything and having a good woman at your side can't be beat."

Zander was right, and a good woman was exactly what he was looking for. "I'll swing by the inn in the morning and pick up that list. Let Quinn know I'll pick her up at eight." He emptied his bottle and set it on the table. "I better get some rest. Tomorrow will be a long day." He'd need to be rested if he was going to be with Quinn for the entire day. She made him twitchy and long for something he couldn't have with her. "Goodnight." He jogged down the steps, careful not to reinjure his knee.

"You good to drive?" Zander called over the railing.

"Yep. One beer stretched over an hour ... I'm good."

Morning came much too early after a long sleepless night. He was more than happy to help his brother out, but he'd prefer to do it alone. At least then he could blast the music in his truck and enjoy the ride instead of making polite conversation.

Quinn was bundled up in a warm jacket with a scarf and toque when she arrived at her doorstep at exactly eight. She opened the door and grinned at him. "Morning, Tyson. How are you this morning?" She hopped up in the truck and buckled up before he could formulate a civil reply.

"Good enough."

"Aren't you excited? I can't wait to shop. I haven't been out of Half Moon Bay for months." She shed her thick mittens and hat. She rubbed her hands together in front of the heater. "Let's do this."

They drove in silence until they turned onto the highway. "What's on the list?" Tyson asked.

"Table linens is the big thing. The inn doesn't have enough of what she needs. With Derrick's plan to host more weddings, they need more than they have."

"Wouldn't it be better for the inn to get that stuff?"

She patted her purse. "I've got the inn's credit card. I know what they want. Derrick and Jacob have given me a budget and specifications."

He grunted. "I'm not much of a shopper."

She looked him up and down. "You're always so well dressed and fashionable."

Somehow the statement felt like a question, so he treated it like one. "I have a shop I go to in Seattle. They've got great staff who understand my needs. I book an appointment, show up, and try things on." He shrugged. "It works. If the outfits are reasonably priced and not hideous, I'm good with it."

"Not hideous? Dude, I saw your Halloween and Christmas sweaters."

Her laughter rang through the truck and was a jolt of unexpected warmth.

"You can thank Mom for those. When she found out the school was having a Halloween costume day, she showed up with the sweater. I wore it under protest. Same for the Christmas one."

"Of course you did. You don't wear a costume?"

"Nope. As an administrator, it appears unprofessional."

"It appears stuffy not to," she corrected with a grin.

"Funny," he grumbled. "Do you really think so?" Her opinion made his chest ache.

"Actually, yes. Even the hospital administrator and all her staff wear costumes. Nothing fancy and no masks or face paint, but they dress up. You should consider it." She was silent for a moment. "Opening yourself up to ridicule might help your students and staff relate to you. You know, make you seem more human?"

"I have until next year to decide." He nodded sharply as if the conversation was done. It should have been a gesture of dismissal, it was for his staff, but Quinn kept on talking.

"Valentine's Day is coming up. So is St. Patrick's Day. I mean, there is something to celebrate every month of the year. I say, go for it, get in there like a hog on lettuce. Dress up. Let your perfectly styled hair down." She laughed. "Metaphorically speaking."

He stewed on her words for longer than he wanted to. He'd always dismissed similar comments from his assistant. He'd taken dozens of managerial courses. Some in person, some online. Her advice went against everything he'd learned. Of course, those classes were a decade or more ago.

"Can we stop for a snack?" she asked. "I'm starved and I need a cup of tea."

He glanced at her. Her cheeks were adorably pink.

"You're blushing because you're hungry?" He shook his head.

She stared out the side window for several minutes. "I have to pee. Okay? Can we just stop? There's a café just up the road here. They have great desserts. I'll get my tea to go."

It had been over a week since their last appointment. He was glad to see she was over her bout of food poisoning. "Come to think of it, I could use a coffee myself."

The stop was short and sweet. Just as he liked them. "I can't believe you're going to eat that." *Especially in my truck*. He glared at the powdered sugar-covered donut in her hand.

"Breakfast of champions," she quipped. "Try it." She thrust it toward him, raining sugar across the armrest.

"No, but thanks." It would take days to clean up that sugar.

"I dare you!"

"No, thank you."

"You're a coward," she taunted. "Afraid of a little sugar? Here's a life tip for you, Ty. Live a little. A bit of sugar won't kill you. Neither will be wearing a costume."

The words rankled. His hackles rose and in a fit of pique, he bit a huge chunk out of the donut she still held in front of him. Heavenly sweetness bathed his tongue and his eyes popped wide. It was delicious! So darn good. He savored every second of the sweet bite melting in his mouth. When had donuts gotten that good?

"Very good." He peered at his face in the rear-view mirror, it was blessedly free of white dust, though his navy sweater hadn't fared so well. It was liberally coated.

"We'll turn you into a human yet," she taunted and nibbled the donut, clearly oblivious to the falling sugar dust.

"I'll have you know that I'm a lean, mean, teaching machine."

"Exactly. You're sub-human. You really do need to lighten up." She wiped her mouth and whispered, "Did you know that you won't get fired for eating a cookie, or, God forbid, for ... smiling at your staff."

"Ha. Ha."

"You'd probably even gain a few friends. Dating might even be possible." There was something in her tone that told him she had something on her mind.

"What are you driving at?" he asked as he pulled out to pass a slow-moving Kenworth.

"Take another bite," she dared.

He wasn't a germaphobe, but sharing food went against his general beliefs. He'd had mono once as a kid, from sharing a soda with his buddy. He bit the donut anyway, surprising them both.

She gasped. "Holy shock therapy." She laughed. "There is a human inside that robot suit."

"Gimme the danged donut," he commanded. She was right. It was the best donut he'd ever eaten, not that he ate many. And it wouldn't kill him to live a little. Occasionally.

"I knew it." She rummaged around in the bag she'd carried out of the café and produced another donut. She gave it to him with a triumphant grin.

"Gloating is not becoming," he said around a mouthful of heavenly goodness.

She laughed, spraying donut and sugar across his dash. "Maybe not, but it's totally happening." She finished her donut and wiped her fingers on a napkin before pulling a package of wet wipes from her oversized purse. She wiped up the dash and dabbed at her clothing.

"Here you go." She handed him a wipe when he finished eating. She reached over and held the wheel, keeping the truck on track while he cleaned up.

He was struck by the memory of his mother doing the same while they were on family road trips in their enormous seven-seater van. "Mom used to hold the wheel for Dad," he said. "She always fixed the wrapper on his burger and handed it to him." The memory warmed him. "She'd hold up his fry cup so he could eat without looking. She was always ready with a napkin for us kids too. I wonder how many meals she ate cold after the rest of us were finished."

"Probably more than one."

"How do you women know to do that?"

"That what?" She stuffed their wipes into the snack bag and folded down the top.

"Look after everyone. Carry wipes in your purse and know when a stop is needed. All of it?"

"Women's intuition?" she asked, her voice landing between seriousness and irreverence.

"I'd have gone hungry until I had time to eat. I didn't even realize I needed coffee, and as much as I hate to admit it, that donut hit the spot. I probably would have stopped at a convenience store and grabbed an apple ... if I stopped at all."

"You do know that all road trip food should be like a kid was given a hundred bucks to spend on junk food, right?"

"Meaning?"

"Road trips should be fun. Blasting music. Unhealthy treats. Too much coffee. Stops at every point of interest, or just to hang out and look at the scenery. I mean, how many times have you even glanced at the stony beaches and the ocean while we've been driving? I'll bet not once."

"A couple of times."

"Liar. I've been watching you. You're eyes to the road every second. Life is meant to be lived, Tyson Bellamie. Don't let it pass you by in your quest for perfection." She picked up her paper takeout cup, flipped open the top, and sipped, eyes closed. "Mm," she exclaimed like she was drinking nirvana itself. "Perfection."

Before he could even think of a response, she returned her cup to the holder, flipped open his, and held it out to him. He blinked in surprise. "Thanks."

"Thanks for stopping," she replied.

He took the cup, sipped, and set it back in the holder. The road ahead was clear, so he risked a glance at her. She stared out the side window, but the tiny bit of her cheek which was visible was pink. Why would giving him a coffee embarrass her? Women were weird.

The morning was shaping up to be beautiful. A few flat, grey clouds, but mostly clear sky. A great day for travel. Traffic was light and the roads clear. Ty let himself steal quick glances at the passing scenery. Quinn was right, he was too focused sometimes. What did that say about him?

Years ago, he'd been a wild pre-teen. Then he stumbled on football. He hadn't wanted to play, but his dad 'encouraged' him to join. Okay, it had been more like 'sign up for football or be grounded for the rest of the school year'. Much to his surprise, he hadn't hated it. Better than that, he'd been good at it. Very good.

He'd been scouted in grade twelve and received a full-ride scholarship. What a ride it had been. With all the practice and games, it had taken him longer than usual to get his degree. A lot of his fellow players hadn't bothered but his dad's voice had rung in his ears, "Get your degree, son. Life throws curves and when you land on your ass, you better have a backup plan."

His parents hadn't been too controlling. But that advice had served him well. As had his mother's to save his money and not fritter it away. He snorted.

"What?" Quinn asked quietly.

"Just thinking about parental advice."

"How so?"

She seemed genuinely interested so he told her about his father. "I was laughing at mom's advice. The last thing she said to me when I left home to play in the big leagues was to keep my dick in my pants."

They laughed together.

"I can totally see her saying that." She paused. "And did you?"

"You better believe it. So many of the football bunnies were after fame, or worse yet, my money. I just wanted to play the game I loved."

"Sorry about your knee." She reached over and patted his arm.

He knew it was an unconscious action on her part, but her empathy touched him. "Thanks. It wasn't anyone's fault. Just stupid dumb luck. But in some ways, it turned out to be a blessing."

"How so? It seems like having your career ruined would be devastating."

"Trust me, it was. But I found a career back home as a Phys-ed teacher and football coach. I loved teaching those kids the joy of the game. And I love helping them through school."

"Do you miss coaching? I know you're the principal now."

"I do. There are days when I wish I could leave the office and work more closely with the students. Of course, I'd also love to be on the school board and help enact serious changes that would benefit the kids."

"Admirable. I like the way you think. I know a lot of kids need solid guidance. I sure did."

"That surprises me." She seemed like she'd always had her life together. "You're so—so organized and capable." He winced at how lame he sounded.

"Thanks. I appreciate it." She sighed. "I was a guidance counselor's nightmare. Lying, cheating, stealing. I had a tough childhood, and I was a nightmare teen."

"What turned you around?"

"It sure wasn't detention. I stole some guy's wheelchair. Biggest mistake and best decision I've ever made." She laughed wryly. "I was busted for theft and forced to do community service. They put me to work in a military rehab clinic. Watching those wounded soldiers, men and women, struggle day by day woke me up, fast. I swear to God, on the second day there, I vowed to help others. And I did."

"I never would have guessed," he said honestly.

"Me either. My folks were astounded."

"Tell me about them." He was growing increasingly curious about her. Her vulnerability in confessing her past shocked and touched him. His heart softened toward her. It hadn't been hard, exactly, but he felt ... differently than he had before.

"Not much to tell. They died while I was in university. Car accident." Her voice dropped to a whisper. "I never got to say goodbye."

He grasped her hand in his. "I am so sorry."

"I've made my peace with it."

She was lying but he didn't call her on it. "Where are they buried?"

"Seattle."

"We could stop and visit them. Take them flowers. If you wanted." The offer was sincere. He'd make time, even staying overnight at his own expense if she wanted to visit.

"Can I think about it?" She turned back toward the side window but didn't pull her hand from his.

He squeezed her hand lightly, and focused on the road, giving her time to grieve. Grieving was a process he knew well. There were days when he'd give anything for five minutes with his father.

They drove, hand in hand until they reached the outskirts of the city, and he needed his entire focus on driving.

Chapter Eight

Quinn wanted to hug herself. Tyson's comfort warmed her right through, and she was going to hold onto that feeling forever. Of course, she'd never have released his hand of her own volition. She gripped his solid strength until he pulled away. She sighed silently and closed her eyes. She committed each precious second to memory. She'd pull them out later and hug them close.

She was already lonely and she'd barely ditched Duke. There was a painful emptiness in knowing that there was no one coming to see you, no date waiting. She hadn't seen Duke often, but there was comfort in knowing he was out there. Though now she wondered if he'd been dating someone else.

Ruthlessly, she shoved the thought aside. She didn't need him. She didn't need any man. Sure, she'd take one. But this time, she was waiting for the right one. She'd love for it to be Tyson. She'd adored him from the first time they met. But she wasn't holding out for him. There were plenty of fish in the sea.

She directed Tyson to the linens company. They had a warehouse on the east end. The parking lot was nearly full, and a handful of employees stood inside a shelter sharing cigarettes and conversation. She held her nose as they hurried past the shelter. She hated that smell.

The receptionist, a thin twenty-something man with a neatly trimmed beard and mustache, greeted them and led them into a small side room.

"Oh, gosh," she exclaimed. "There must be hundreds of colors here."

Tyson groaned.

She swatted his arm. "It won't be that bad."

"That's what she said," he quipped, making her laugh.

She turned to Ted, the receptionist. "Don't mind him, he's just my ride." She threw Tyson a quick wink, so he'd know she was teasing. "Let's get started. Where do we begin, Ted?"

"I received the inn's email, and they plan to start with black, white, emerald, and burgundy napkins. Plus, black and white table-cloths. Let's start there." He waved them to the end of the table. "We've got two basic styles. Plain and with a decorative border on two sides." He placed one of each in her hands.

The decorative border was a simple change in texture on the opposite edges. It was very subtle.

"What do you think, Tyson?"

"I think a napkin is for wiping your face." He rolled his eyes. "You said it yourself, I'm just your driver."

"Funny. Not. Have an opinion."

He looked the answer over. "What's the price differential between the two styles and what is the long-term availability if the inn needs to re-order?"

Quinn gaped at him. She hadn't even thought of those questions. She grinned at him and turned to Ted with a raised eyebrow.

"They're all stock items. We've carried them for years. The trimmed ones are slightly more expensive." He laid out the cost difference.

"What's the durability difference?" Tyson asked.

"Equivalent." Ted seemed surprised by Tyson's wise questions.

Quinn was, and wasn't, surprised. He was intelligent. He had to be, or he'd never have been made school principal. Plus, rumor had it that he'd made wise investments with his money. He also played in the weekly Scrabble tournament at the library. He'd always had a quick turn of phrase or fast joke while they trained together. She missed those days already.

"I say we go with the edged ones. What do you think?" She turned her full attention to him. The room's fluorescent lights highlighted his hair and beard and made his eyes shine. She was struck, as she was every time she saw him, with how attractive he was. Her heart thumped, and she squeezed her hands into fists to keep from reaching out and stroking his cheek.

He stared at her for a moment and cleared his throat. "Sure. As long as they'll be available in the future."

"Perfect." Ted made a note on his tablet. "I have the colors and quantities already. Would you like to take those today or shall we ship them?"

"Let's ship the bulk of the order. But we'll need to take the specialty linens today."

He made another note. "Okay, down here, we have all our colors. They're divided into two groups. Those on the left," he gestured, "are only available in limited quantities and won't be replaceable. On the right are standard stock."

There had to be two hundred choices. Many were the same color but available in different fabric weights.

"Which are the most durable?" she asked.

"Good question," Tyson said. She jerked backward and bumped into him. She hadn't heard him step up behind her. She took half a second to enjoy the heat of his chest against her back before she moved away.

She had trouble focusing on the discussion. Tyson's light spice scent lingered in her nostrils, and she found herself leaning toward him again and again.

"Well?" Tyson looked at her. "What do you think?"

"Right!" She rummaged in her purse and pulled out a plastic zipper bag. "Let's compare with these scraps." She pulled a six-inch strip of fabric from the bag.

"What's that?" Tyson nodded toward the fabric.

"It's a scrap from the bridesmaid dresses. Heather wants to make sure we don't clash with the table wear."

"Women."

She jabbed him with her elbow. "Heather's my best friend and I want her wedding to be perfect. I'd think you'd want the same for your brother."

"You aren't the bride and groom?" Ted sounded surprised. "I thought you were, judging by the sparks between you."

Tyson reared back. "Nope. Just friends."

Ouch! That hurt.

"Just friends," she repeated sadly. So much for the handholding.

"My apologies." Ted bowed slightly.

"No problem." She started shuffling through the colors and gathered a few in her hands. "Do you have a white tablecloth?"

"Certainly, give me a moment." He hustled out of the room.

She stood beside Tyson, searching for something to say and wondering how Ted had noticed her attraction. She thought she did a good job of keeping it secret. Apparently not. Ty seemed equally unable to speak.

Ted bustled back in and with a flutter of fabric he draped the pristine cloth over the pile of napkins. "Here you go, dear."

Dear? She squinted at him. Tyson glared. *Interesting.* Forcing herself back to the task, she laid out the napkins she'd pulled from the pile and placed the fabric strips across the ends.

Some of the fabrics clashed horribly with her selections. Others blended right in. None of them were right. "They suck," she whined, tapping her finger on her lips.

"What about peach? Or navy?" Tyson said.

She whirled to face him. "What? Are you nuts?"

He laughed. "Probably. But the green reminds me of leaves. Mom has these amazing peach roses that bloom all summer." He walked around the table, shifting napkins and gathering a few different ones. He came back with three shades of blue and two of peach. He spread them in a fan on the white cloth and shifted her fabric over.

"Dang it." Every choice was perfect. They all matched. "They're great. I might hate you right now." She grinned.

He chuckled and then laughed so hard he was gasping. "You're hilarious," he choked out between chuckles. She joined in laughing. Ted glared at them like they were insane.

Finally, she was able to catch her breath. She looked away from Tyson. If she looked at him, she'd crack up again. It probably wasn't funny, but somehow it was. She picked out a peach and a navy. "We'll take a standard order of each of these, with the decorative edge."

"That's a lot," Ty warned her.

"It's what Heather asked for. Two choices, a full complement of each. We'll take navy tablecloths as well. The peach will look divine on the navy. And the navy will work on white."

Tyson winced.

"They're thinking of getting into the wedding business. Heather is already catering several weddings in the community center and there is talk of expanding the inn with a wedding venue. Think destination wedding. It would be a boon for the entire town."

"How did I miss all that?"

"It's not public yet. Heather mentioned it when I asked why so many linens." She turned to Ted. "We'll take the navy and peach napkins, and the navy tablecloths today. I'll pay for them now. Can you ship the rest?"

"Are you certain on the peach? It's not our most popular, and there are no returns," Ted warned.

"We're certain," Tyson replied in a very no-nonsense voice. "We'll pay now and stop back later to pick them up."

Tyson took her arm and led her out of the room. "Wiener," he whispered under his breath. "As if you're not smart enough to know what you need."

She giggled. Ted was okay, but a bit pompous. They waited in the lobby while Ted tallied their order. Quinn paid by card and before she knew it, Tyson had her by elbow and was steering her outside.

"Watch your step," he warned. "There's a bit of ice."

She glanced around and saw water, but no ice. Still, she let him guide her to the truck, waited while he opened the door, and used his outstretched hand for support to climb in. She smiled at him as he eased her door shut. *What was that all about?*

Chapter Nine

Tyson fumed at himself. What was he doing being all friendly and protective of Quinn? They weren't a thing. They were barely friends. Ted's disdain had rankled. How dare he insinuate Quinn didn't know what she was doing? Thinking it was one thing, but to say it? *Argh.*

He glanced at Quinn as he climbed in. She had an adorable, cat-who-ate-the-cream smile that made him grin.

For half a second, he wondered why she looked so pleased. Then it dawned on him. Duke wasn't likely much for compliments, or proper care of a woman. He was more the beer chugging, belching, quick roll in the hay type.

Well, he'd show Quinn how she deserved to be treated. How all women deserved to be treated. With kindness and respect.

She'd soon know that she was worthy of a better man than Duke Farnsworth.

"Where too, m'lady?" He mock bowed and slipped the truck into gear.

"There's an order to pick up at a shop not far from here. Take a left at the street coming up."

Slowly, battling the surprisingly heavy late morning traffic, they wended their way north and then west. He parked in the lot of a small strip mall in front of a place called Frannie's.

"Why don't you wait in the truck?" she suggested.

"I'll come in and carry your packages."

"Um. You should probably wait here." Her cheeks turned pink.

Women were adorable, but so weird. "I'll come in." She had him curious now. What was inside the innocuous looking shop that would embarrass a woman. The windows displayed what he assumed were fashionable dresses though they were too flashy for his tastes. "Let's go."

"It's your funeral. Don't say I didn't warn you."

He pulled open the shop door. A bell tinkled lightly over muted strains of instrumental music. They were greeted with racks of dresses similar to those in the window. The place had a serious, reverent air ... until wild laughter broke out near the back of the store.

Quinn pushed past the first tall racks, and he followed. They stepped into a man's worst nightmare.

Lingerie!

In every imaginable color. Satin, silk, ribbons, lace. Oh God, so much lace! His face heated. He nailed his boots to the floor. He wasn't bolting. He was tougher than that.

"Oh look," Quinn whispered as she fingered a decidedly sexy black and red lace … What did he even call that thing? It wasn't pajamas. It was more than a bra and panties., but not that exactly.

He swallowed hard. Holy hell. He was in trouble. This was fantasy heaven. Who knew heaven and hell were so close together? He was struck dumb by a sudden vision of Quinn wearing that … that thing.

Whew! He was sweating.

Was it getting hot in here?

Down boy! Respect for women. Play it cool. You should have listened to her. Seriously. You're an idiot. Go back to the truck.

As much as he was mortified, he was equally intrigued and stayed put.

He watched, dumbstruck and practically drooling as Quinn moved from rack to rack. She pulled out outfits, examined them, tilted her head this way and that, and put them back. But not before he was blinded by visions of her in those delicious confections. Whoever invented lingerie was a jerk. A total jerk. A brilliant one too.

Quinn rarely wore tight clothing, but he'd seen her legs more than once while working out. She'd kill in those outfits. It was enough to give a man a heart attack.

She pulled out a slender, wispy thing in bright pink. Fuchsia. That's what his mom would call it. She held it against herself and looked down.

His heartbeat skyrocketed and he gasped. Jeepers!

She whirled around. "Are you okay?" She rushed up to him and grasped his hand. The silky fabric brushed his arm and his mind whirled away to an unmentionable place.

"Tyson. Ty? Are you okay?"

He tried to speak past the lump of desire in his face. He choked and swallowed hard. "Ya. Ya. I'm good. Thirsty." Hungry was more like it. Hungry for Quinn.

A pretty young woman walked up to them. Tall and slender, she wore a demure dress, just the type he liked. Objectively Ty knew she was lovely. Beside Quinn, she looked like a rusty Honda next to a Porsche.

"We get that from a lot of men." She laughed. The sound grated on his nerves. "I'll grab you a water. Or would you prefer a latte?"

"Water's good." He had to grunt the words out.

"What is wrong with you?" Quinn whispered, her minty breath warm on his cheek. "Haven't you ever seen lingerie before?"

"Not like this." Nothing in his entire life had prepared him for this ... this attack on his heart and libido.

"Huh." She grinned. "I've got a dresser full of the stuff. Wear it all the time." She wandered away, leaving him staring at her back. Dang long coat hid the view too. This sucked. He was hooked from the moment they entered the store. And he would be until the second he managed to get back into the truck. He couldn't leave now.

Quinn turned back toward him. "Feel free to go back to the truck." She grinned impudently.

He stomped up to her. "Not on your fricken life. Baby, I'm all in."

"Oh? Good. Maybe you can help me pick out something sexy for under my bridesmaid dress."

"Count on it," he growled. It would give him erotic dreams for weeks, but he wasn't backing down.

Five minutes later, he regretted that decision, but not enough to leave. He followed Quinn and two salesclerks around as they pulled wispy confections off racks and held them up for inspection.

Everything from micro bras to thongs. Full size, tiny, in between, and in all colors under the rainbow.

Quinn took several sets into a curtained alcove near the back. Unsure what to do with himself, he took a seat outside the alcove and prayed that she didn't come out in those bits of nothing.

His prayers were answered, she remained hidden by the curtain. As she handed items out and asked for different sizes, his imagination was more than eager to provide unwanted images of Quinn in lingerie. He closed his eyes and willed his thoughts to things he needed to do for work.

He wasn't even slightly effective at distracting himself. Especially not when the salesclerk exclaimed, "Oh, that's perfect. You'll drive your man wild in that. The emerald green is perfect on you. And that lace highlights everything."

"I'll take it," Quinn said. "And these."

An eternity later, they slid her package and Heather's box of stuff under the tonneau cover of his truck. His heart was still pounding, and his imagination was still busy providing visuals of things best left unseen by a single man. He wasn't a prude, but certain things were meant for married men, not bachelors. Especially since he had no intention of dating Quinn.

Friends. That's what they were, and he wasn't going to alter that status.

Chapter Ten

Quinn climbed into the truck, trying to hide her grin. She'd warned him to wait. She winced a bit at the hit to her tight budget, but shopping had been irresistible when he followed her. It was time Tyson Bellamie realized that she was a living, breathing woman worthy of consideration.

She wanted to laugh at the shock on his face, and the fact that he absolutely couldn't hide his interest. It was probably mean to tease him by taking so long to buy things she didn't need, but the rush of power she got from his interest was satisfying and invigorating.

It took him a full minute to join her in the truck. He stood by the end gate, his back to the truck until she wondered if she'd have to ask him to get in. Finally, he climbed in and started the engine.

"Where to, boss lady?" He cleared his throat and buckled up.

They hit two stores for wedding party favors Heather had pre-ordered at the last minute. With all the events happening at the inn, she'd been too distracted to remember her own wedding.

Quinn and Heather had talked for hours on Heather's last evening off. They decided what was needed for the wedding and Heather had ordered it. Being Heather's bridesmaid was fun and painful all at once. There was a lot of work left to do and today's trip wasn't the last of it. But helping her best friend was more pleasure than work. Especially when she got to spend time with Tyson.

"I appreciate you driving today. I know Heather's very grateful too."

He grunted. "No problem." He stared straight ahead at Frannie's display window, a confused expression on his face.

"Are you okay?" she asked.

He grunted again. Apparently, he was turning neanderthal. "I'm hungry."

"There's a great family-owned restaurant about ten blocks from here."

Ten minutes later she was studying the menu looking for something that didn't turn her stomach. She was seriously thinking about going to the doctor. Her stomach was up and down every day. Right now, she was ravenous, but nothing appealed.

"What are you having?" she asked.

"The whole wheat pasta with lemon, garlic sauce. It will be light and healthy. I'll add some shrimp and a small green salad. How about you? What looks good?"

"Not pasta, that's for sure." She smiled at him, unable to help herself. She flipped through the multi-page menu discarding breakfast and burger options. She settled on an order of perogies and sausage. Hold the sauerkraut.

They talked about the wedding while eating. She finished her meal and was still hungry. "Are you going to eat that garlic toast?"

"No. I forgot to cancel it. I'm reducing my white bread intake. Would you like it?"

"Yes!" She reached over and snatched it off his plate. "I'm still hungry. Do you mind if I order dessert? I'm paying for my own meal," she added before he had time to misconstrue her question as a bid for him to pick up the check.

"Help yourself." He slid the upright dessert sheet toward her. "I'll pass, but you go ahead. I'm just going to have another coffee."

She tried not to feel self-conscious as she ate, but he stared at her the entire time. Finally, she thrust a forkful of cherry-cream filled chocolate cake at him. "Taste this, it's divine. Best cake I ever had." She laughed. "Don't tell Heather I said that."

He eyed the fork suspiciously. "I don't eat sweets."

"We've had this discussion already. Live a little. A single taste won't turn you into a marshmallow man you know. Try it, Tyson. I dare you."

He squinted at her and for a second, she could have sworn she saw the corner of his mouth turn up in a hint of a smile. She pushed the fork closer. "I dare you," she sing-songed.

He took the bite. She could tell he was savoring it and enjoying it a lot. "It is good."

She slid the plate closer. "Have some." The piece was huge. She'd barely eaten a third of it. She was planning on getting a doggy bag for the rest, but if he wanted it, she'd share for sure.

There was something very pleasant about corrupting the straightlaced Tyson Bellamie. Sure, it was only a treat here and there, but he could use loosening up. Maybe he'd become more flexible and more human. Maybe if he relaxed enough, he'd consider her date worthy.

He ate three small bites and set his fork down. "That's enough for me." He patted his flat stomach. "I have to stay fit."

Feeling called out, she ate a few more bites before asking for a box. "I could eat the entire thing," she lied. "But I'll get the rest to go so we can finish up. I have things to do at home." She didn't, but Tyson didn't need to know that.

"Oh. Okay."

"What does that mean?" She asked.

"I had a random thought. There's a *Star Trek* movie marathon playing on a cable channel I don't get. I was debating getting a hotel room and watching it."

"You want to stay in town all night?" She adored *Star Trek*. If it wasn't for her budget, she'd be all in with staying.

"I'd pay for your room," he offered.

"I couldn't let you do that. Why don't we stay? I am off tomorrow, and I love Kirk."

"Sulu and Chekov are far superior characters. Let me check out some hotels and make sure they have the channel we need." He pulled out his phone and began his search.

She sipped her herbal tea and waited. Their server came and took the cake for boxing and returned it. He was still looking. He started typing, pulled out his wallet and credit card, and typed some more. Finally, he looked up. "Done. Reservation made. Is there anything you need to do before we check in? We've got ninety minutes before the marathon starts."

"Maybe we could hit a big box store. I'll need toiletries and some pjs." And a few other things, but he didn't really need a list.

"Done. I know the perfect shop and it's on the way."

An hour later, they parked in the hotel's underground lot. "I booked a suite. Two bedrooms and a main seating area. Complete with kitchenette for snack preparation."

They were sharing a room. That was almost like staying together. Or sharing an apartment. Her pulse thrummed in her ears, growing louder as her heartbeat accelerated. Wasn't that against his moral code?

"Are you sure sharing is a good idea? I mean ... your reputation?"

"It'll be fine. We're not in Half Moon Bay. Nobody will see us. There are separate bedrooms. Plus, the suite saved me nearly ninety dollars over the cost of two rooms."

"I'm paying for my share. Let me e-transfer you."

"No, thanks though. This is on me. It was my idea."

She couldn't stop herself from asking one more time. "Please let me contribute." It wasn't in her to pay less than her full share. She believed in pulling her own weight.

"Is this going to be an issue?" He turned toward her, a deep frown on his face. "I'm considering this as you doing me a favor. I wanted to binge some old TV and you're putting up with my obsession. Can we please just let it drop? You can pay for dinner if we order anything." He gave her a does-that-suit-you look.

She rolled her eyes. *Men! Ugh.* "That makes me feel better, yes."

"Fine. Let's go in. I want to be settled before the show starts." He climbed out of the truck and opened the back door. "Hang on a second." He carted some things to the back and tucked them under the locking cover. "Here, stick your bags into my emergency bag. I don't want you to feel all weird while we check in."

"Thanks." She'd been debating checking in empty handed but wasn't sure if that would be worse than with shopping bags. Realistically, nobody would think twice about a couple checking in with shopping bags, but she worried they'd think she was having an affair with Tyson if they had nothing. She sighed. She did tend to overthink things. The desk staff had probably seen everything, and this wasn't exactly a dive. While it wasn't top end, it was more than respectable.

They rode the elevator to the lobby. The doors opened to a large marble foyer. Far across the expanse, a gleaming wood and brass check-in desk loomed. Scattered across the space were plush gray chairs. Everything was gray and cream and polished wood. Their footsteps echoed across the wide space. Thank heaven she wasn't wearing heels, or she'd be clumping across.

A young dark-haired man in a navy suit greeted them at the desk. "Good afternoon. I'm Evan. How can I help you today?" His smile was cool and blended welcome and condescension.

"Tyson Bellamie. Nice to meet you. We're checking in."

"Tyson Bellamie? Former football star?" Evan's expression changed from disinterested to a genuine smile.

"Yes. That's me. I'm a high school principal now. I've retired."

"I remember that hit. Danged shame about your career," Evan commiserated. "I was a huge fan." He leaned left a bit to look at Quinn. "I assume this is your wife?"

"No. A business associate. We're here for my brother's inn."

Business associate? I guess that's okay. I'm certainly not his wife though I wouldn't turn down the position.

"We'll need her information," Evan said.

Tyson fixed him with a stare that would have melted steel. Quinn suppressed a smirk as the man paled. "And would you ask my wife, if I had one, to provide ID?"

The man reared back in shock. "I'll just need a credit card to bill to." Suddenly, he was back to being all business. He took Tyson's information and credit card and slid two electronic keys over the counter.

In a manner unlike the Tyson she was used to, he fumed all the way to the elevator and up to their suite.

"I can't believe he pried into my life like that. Who I am with is none of his business. There was no reason for him to learn your name. He's just looking for gossip." He continued to grumble until they stood outside their door.

She placed her hand on his forearm as he reached out with the key. "Ty? It's okay. It really is. No harm done. He was just a fan and wanted to know more about you. Relax, okay?"

"It annoys me. I thought I was through with all that crap." He swiped the card too quickly and it flashed red. He swiped again. And again.

"Hey, let me try." She pried the card out of his tight fingers and slowly slid it through the track. "I'm surprised they don't use the lock where you just press the card to it or slip it into a slot until it beeps." She opened the door and stepped inside. She held it so he could enter behind her.

He walked past and she eased the door shut before turning to look at the room. "Wow! This place is sweet!" She kicked off her shoes and strode through the seating room and pulled back the sheer curtains. "You can see the ocean," she pointed. "This is amazing." Being near the ocean wasn't new, but she couldn't recall ever seeing it from fifteen floors up. What a game changer!

She spun around. Like the lobby downstairs, the sitting area was decorated neutrally, but a bouquet of fresh flowers sat atop a bar. Glasses hung from a rack above that. This area was more like an apartment than a hotel room. Aside from the entry, two doors branched off the main room, one to each side. She peeked into one, then the other to find two equal-sized bedrooms, each with its own bathroom. She flopped onto her back on the second bed.

Firm but soft and very comfortable. She wanted to burrow in for a nap.

"Will it do?" Tyson asked from the doorway.

"Oh gosh. Yes. It's lovely and wonderful. I've never stayed in a place this nice. I'm more a budget hotel type of girl." She popped up and grinned at him. "Thanks for this."

He nodded. "You're very welcome. You take this room. I'll take the other." His smile was soft and pleased looking. It tickled something deep inside her heart.

She rubbed her hands together. "Let the marathon begin." She laughed when he echoed her sentiment.

Tyson sat in the side chair while Quinn curled up on the loveseat. There was probably room for both of them, but he didn't want to crowd her. Being this close to her seemed almost too intimate for him. She likely felt the same though her objections to staying over had been more about teasing him for his reputation. Had she been right to fret? He sighed. Too late now, they were here, it was the middle of the night, and she was fast asleep. She'd dozed off half a movie earlier.

His gaze was drawn to her again and again. Occasionally, he'd caught her looking at him with a soft secretive smile on her face. She was adorable, all curled up in a ball, her hands tucked under her chin. She wore navy yoga pants and an oversized T-shirt, and her feet were bare. The room was warm but as he watched her, she cuddled into a tighter ball. He grabbed an extra blanket from the dresser in his room and draped it over her, tucking her in carefully, especially those adorable, red-tipped toes.

He recalled coming home from an outing with his father and brothers. Their mom was fast asleep on the sofa when they tumbled through the front door. His dad hushed them, tiptoed into the room, and draped a blanket over her before herding them back outside. They'd gone out for dinner and brought her home her favorite treats. Eating in restaurants wasn't common for them, so it was a treat for everyone. His mom raved for weeks about how sweet it had been to wake up after a long, much-needed nap to find herself covered up.

His dad had talked about how easy it was to do things for the people you loved. Simple things. Honest things. Looking at Quinn right now, he understood what his father meant to a much greater depth than he had when he was eleven.

He frowned. He was starting to care for Quinn. He'd always appreciated her skill as a physiotherapist. She had a great bedside manner and a light, fun sense of humor. She could give a verbal jab but take one as well. She'd been a riot tonight, pointing out plot holes, quoting dialog, or making up new lines that fit just as well, sometimes better. Her childlike pleasure in the hotel room made it worth every second it had taken him to find a decent suite, and every penny of the cost. Alone, he'd have stayed somewhere much more economical. If he stayed at all.

He sat watching the rise and fall of her chest as she slept. She wiggled a bit, and a soft smile graced her pretty pink lips. He should go to bed, but somehow, he couldn't drag himself from the room.

The distant sound of a couple arguing woke him. He jerked upright. His neck ached. He'd fallen asleep. Quinn slept on, undisturbed. He took a moment to be sure there wasn't anything seriously amiss with the couple in the hall, then twisted his neck back and forth to relieve the ache, and reluctantly sought his bed.

Chapter Eleven

Quinn hurried into the church. She was running late. Heather would be beside herself with worry, and Quinn did not want to ruin her best friend's wedding day. She'd woken early with an upset stomach and been floored by the sudden realization that she was probably pregnant. Fear, hope, and happiness battled for supremacy in her heart. Anxiety almost made her sick again.

"Buck up, Davidson," she encouraged herself. "You can figure it out on Monday. Today is Heather's day."

If only it was that easy to discard the idea of carrying a child. She stared at herself in the bathroom mirror. "You've got this kid. Ya, in more ways than one."

She was losing her best friend as a roommate today and was probably a pregnant single mother. No way on earth could she give up her child, even though her sweet baby came from Duke. There was no way she'd even tell Duke about her pregnancy. He likely wouldn't believe her anyway; besides most days he could barely keep himself alive, let alone take on another responsibility. Nope. She'd manage just fine, thank you very much.

She regretted sleeping with him that last time. Heck, she regretted every time. Now that she'd been around Tyson so much with wedding prep and physio, she knew what a man should be like. She should have kicked Duke out that last night instead of letting him come in.

That was all water under the bridge. She was moving on now. Maybe not steadily, but with a strong and loving heart. She'd do her best for this child. Right after she did her best for Heather and Zander's wedding.

"Hey, sorry I'm late," she declared as she entered the back room in the church where Heather was getting ready. Zander's mom, Beth, was there to help Heather into her dress. Sammi and Lexi, the two other bridesmaids were also there. As was Lexi's daughter Ella. Everyone looked amazing.

"Quinn, you're pale. Are you still unwell?" Heather asked.

"A bit under the weather. I've got an appointment to see the doctor next week. I'm good to go, so don't worry about me. Let's make this day perfect."

Heather gave her a questioning look, and she shot back 'a don't ask' look. After a few seconds, her friend nodded. There would be questions later, after the honeymoon. Well, that gave her a full two weeks to figure things out. By the time Heather got back, Quinn would know for sure if she was pregnant, and she'd have a plan in place for dealing with it. Thank heaven she had a large savings account. She'd probably have to delay opening her own physiotherapy business, but that was life.

Life. She was tempted to place her hands on her belly and see if there were any changes. She held herself in check. No sense alerting Heather to the possibility. She hung her dress bag on a rack in the corner and hurried to Heather's side.

"You look amazing." Heather's makeup was complete, her hair styled in a sexy updo and decorated with glittering pins. She was ready to put her dress on. "Let's get you into your dress, then I'll get into mine." Everyone else was ready.

Heather's dress was a slim fitting silk sheath with glittering jewels dabbed here and there. It accentuated her slim figure without being too tight. It widened slightly near the floor giving it a dramatic feel. It suited her personality perfectly.

Between fretting over Heather's outfit, getting into her own, and intruding thoughts of being pregnant, it seemed like only seconds before it was time to enter the sanctuary for the ceremony. She stepped out into the hallway to let Tyson know they were ready.

He was pacing back and forth in the small hallway. She scanned him head to toe, taking in his glorious perfection. Neatly trimmed beard, dark tux, and tie. He was breathtaking. "Hi." She swallowed a lump in her throat. She'd be dancing with him later. Her heart thumped and her stomach rolled with excited anticipation. "We're ready whenever everyone else is."

"Quinn." He swallowed. "You look very nice."

Heat flooded her cheeks. "Thanks. You do too."

He stared at her for a long moment. She grew hotter with every second.

Finally, he shook his head. "Okay. I'll get everyone in place and tell the organist to start. Two minutes." He turned to go, then turned back. "You really do look nice." He scurried away.

She watched until he rounded the corner. She fanned her face to dispel some heat and went back into the room. Beth hurried to take her seat. It seemed an eternity until the music started. A slow, stately piece played and would change to the wedding march when Heather stepped into the doorway to the sanctuary.

Heather had decreed the order to go up the aisle. As maid of honor, Quinn went first. Tyson was acting as father of the bride and best man and would accompany Heather down the aisle.

Quinn took a deep breath. She wasn't shy, but walking up the aisle first was nerve-wracking. Still, she couldn't help but wish this were her wedding. She moved slowly as they had practiced. Zander stood beside the minister. His brothers, Derrick and Jacob stood to his side.

Zander looked calm and eager as he waited for his bride. Derrick looked uncomfortable in his suit, and Jacob appeared like this was just another day. A businessman through and through, being up front didn't faze him one bit.

Quinn took her place as Sammi came up the aisle, her eyes on Derrick, the love of her life. Lexi was equally besotted with Jacob. When it was her turn, young Ella hesitated at the threshold. Even from the front of the church, her deep inhalation was noticeable. The teen was obviously nervous. Her spine straightened and she strode forward. When she reached the front, she grasped her mother's hand and whispered, "Whew."

The music morphed to the Wedding March and all heads turned to the rear. Heather, on Tyson's arm, stepped into view and everyone gasped. She was absolutely glowing. Tyson looked proud to be at her side.

Quinn couldn't tear her eyes from Tyson. He was stunning. Strong, powerful, a slight smile curving his lips, he was masculine perfection, and her heart cried out for him. Much too quickly, they reached the front and stopped beside the last pew.

"Who gives this woman to be wed," the minister asked.

"We do!" The entire Bellamie family called in unison.

A ripple of amusement passed through the crowd and the ceremony began.

It was probably lovely. Quinn couldn't say for sure. She could barely keep her eyes off Tyson. The next thing she knew, Zander dipped Heather low and kissed her until all the guests cheered.

Finally, at long last, the rest of the party was retreating down the aisle. She placed her hand in Tyson's crooked elbow, and they moved toward the exit.

"That was lovely," she said as if she'd been paying attention.

"They'll be happy together," he said with a strong certain voice. "They're very much in love." He sighed. "I want that someday."

"Me too," she agreed. *With you*, she added in her head. As if Mr. Reputation would ever have anything to do with her. He hadn't wanted her before and certainly wouldn't now that she was pregnant.

They joined the crowd outside in the chill February air. Luckily, it was a bright sunny day. After a few minutes, Ty slipped his jacket off and draped it over her shoulders. "You'll freeze without sleeves."

"Thanks. I am chilly."

Time seemed to be dragging. Pictures took an eternity. Dinner was long and drawn out. The guests seemed to be enjoying themselves. The bride and groom were ecstatic. Quinn just wanted to get to the part when the members of the wedding party danced together.

Finally, the happy couple danced and invited their party members to join in and she was in Tyson's arms. Heather had arranged it so Quinn would dance with Tyson. She knew that Quinn had a thing for her future brother-in-law.

They floated around the dance floor to a slow waltz. She was in absolute heaven. He smelled of cedar and spice. His strong arms guided her with gentle care. His warm hand warmed her cold one, while the other warmed her hip. Bliss. Pure, sweet, bliss.

The dance was over before it started. They went their separate ways and visited with old friends and new. Late in the evening, she was seated talking to Tyson's family when Derrick swooped in and stole Sammi for a dance, and Jacob stole Lexi. Beth danced with Ella. Quinn was left alone with Tyson as the band announced the final dance of the evening.

He stood and offered his hand. "Care for the last dance?"

Her heartbeat tripled. "Sure."

She recorded every step into her memory. Every turn, swirl, and heartbeat. She wasn't going to be dating anytime soon. She'd need tonight's memories to keep her warm over the coming months. She sighed, part bliss, part sadness.

"That's a deep sigh. Are you tired?"

"A bit. Melancholy too. I'm losing a roommate. My life is changing and I'm not sure I'm ready for it."

"You'll find another roommate. Maybe someone from the hospital," he consoled.

"I've got one in mind already." Her heart glowed with love for her unborn child. Weird. She was in love with a child whose existence she hadn't even confirmed.

"That's a good thing. You'll be okay." He spun her in a slow circle.

"You know what? I will be okay. Thanks for reminding me."

The band morphed into an unexpected waltz. She didn't mention it and neither did he. They danced as if nothing had changed. Much too quickly, it was over. Her heart wept as he stepped back.

"Can I give you a ride home?"

"I brought my car." She should have taken a cab, but she'd been behind schedule.

"I don't feel right letting you go home alone this late. Let me drive you," he insisted.

She wanted to say no, but she couldn't. "Thank you. I'd love a ride. I can come back tomorrow for my car."

"I'll get my truck and meet you out front." He left her standing at the edge of the dance floor watching the band take down their equipment.

She wrapped her arms around herself and cuddled into the warmth of knowing she'd have a few more minutes time with him.

The ride home was too short. "Would you like some tea?" she blurted when he pulled to a stop at her apartment.

"If you have herbal."

"I do." Just like that he was following her inside. She felt a bit like a spider luring a fly into its web.

Chapter Twelve

E ven as he climbed the stairs behind Quinn, Tyson knew this was a mistake. For his own sanity, he'd cut their physio short by a couple of weeks, he'd avoided her at every turn. Then they'd spent an entire day and an evening together in the city. He'd danced with her more than the single required time. He was trying to stay away from her and here he was traipsing up the stairs to her apartment for tea.

He didn't need tea. He needed a beer and a good dose of reality. And maybe some willpower to go with it. She was irresistible.

"The wedding was lovely," Quinn said as she unlocked the door. "Don't you think?"

"It was a wedding."

"Such a guy response," she teased. "What wasn't nice?"

"I didn't say it wasn't nice. It was just like any other, except I had to take part and not just watch. Eating in front of a crowd on a raised platform was nerve-wracking. I was terrified I was going to spill something on my suit."

"Me too. I don't like crowds to start with, but eating on stage was the worst." He laughed at her dramatic shudder.

"Why do people have big weddings? Most of my college buddies had big events and they're all divorced. Do you think there's a correlation?"

"What? No way." She shed her jacket and shoes and padded into the kitchen. "It's a relief to be out of those heels." She filled the kettle. "I think that marriage isn't easy. It takes work. People fight. They have different opinions and needs change. You have to muddle through it all the time. My grandmother told me marriage is 100% all the time." She turned to look at him.

Their gazes meshed. "She said sometimes you give 100%, sometimes you take 100%. The secret to a good marriage is knowing that and being okay with it. Life will balance out if you focus on doing the best for your partner and your relationship. And avoid listening to the gossips and Negative Nellies and be honest with each other."

It took him several moments to unwrap her statements. There was a lot there. He pondered his parents' relationship. It strongly resembled what she said. He'd even caught his mother talking to her deceased husband, more than once. Gently, he'd called her on it, worried about her sanity. Laughing, she'd told him that she missed her husband and talking to him helped her worry out her problems just as it did when they were married.

He kept the revelations to himself. He didn't want to overshare. He was trying to keep his distance. He nodded. "Makes sense."

"Lemon mint? Decaf Earl Gray, Sleepy, peppermint, or orange spice?" She turned away and pulled a decorative box from a lower cupboard. She flipped it open and looked at him.

"Orange spice?"

"Don't sound so certain," she teased. "There is no wrong answer."

He laughed with her. "Orange spice, please and thank you. Nothing in it."

She made the tea and poured them generous mugs full. "Let's sit in the living room. It's more comfortable."

He'd been here before, with Zander. He knew the layout. He sat at one end of the bright red, three-seater couch and she took the other. She sat with her back against the armrest, her feet tucked under a blanket, facing him. They stared at each other.

A minute went by.

Then two.

The silence was stretching too long and becoming uncomfortable. He cleared his throat.

She cleared hers. "Want to play a game?"

"What kind of game?" he asked warily.

"Would you rather?"

"Would I rather what?" he asked, squeezing the mug between his fingers. He was so out of his element. This wasn't like dating when there was an end goal. It wasn't like friendship where there was no goal. It was just weird.

She laughed for a full minute. "Not like that." She chuckled a bit more. "The game is would you rather. I ask you a question. You answer it. You can ask me the same question, or a different one."

He nodded his comprehension. "So ... modified truth or dare? Okay, I'm game." Anything to break the uncomfortable silence and his growing need to move closer to her.

"Would you rather be a dog or a cat?"

He answered without hesitation. "That's easy. A dog. I'd be a protector. Cats are lazy and cold-hearted. How about you?" The game was odd, but interesting.

"Oh, a cat for sure. I love dozing in the sun and sleeping. I love how they stretch, and it involves their entire body." She sipped her tea and licked a drop off her lip. He stared at her mouth. Her lips moved.

"Sorry, what? I was distracted for a second."

Her grin was full Cheshire cat.

Busted.

"I said, would you rather take a beach vacation, or go skiing?"

"Do I have to choose one of those? Can I pick visit some Mayan ruins instead?" Beach vacations held little appeal. He wasn't a skier since he'd injured himself. He was a learner. He liked to keep his mind occupied. Historic places were right up his alley.

"I'll take that answer."

"Would you rather have one child or two?" The question popped out unbidden.

"Wow. That escalated quickly. Four, maybe five. I want a big family." She jabbed a thumb toward her chest. "Only child here. I want siblings for my kids. And, if I had a choice, I'd marry into a big family. One with lots of aunts and uncles for my kids. A strong support network."

Like the night they'd sat in the truck talking, and again in their hotel room, they fell into easy conversation. The game popped up again now and then, but mostly they chatted.

She yawned widely. "Oh gosh. I'm tired. It just hit me suddenly."

He jumped up. "I should go. I've kept you up too late already." He checked his watch. "Holy smokes. It's almost five. We've got that post wedding, family brunch and gift opening thing in a couple hours."

"Thanks for bringing me home." She stood and stretched.

He almost salivated at her slim curves still wrapped in the silken fabric of her bridesmaid dress. It was a bit wrinkled, and her hair was falling from its fancy updo, but she was still gorgeous.

"You're welcome. It was my pleasure. I guess I'll see you in a little while." Reluctantly, he put on his shoes. Hand on the doorknob he said, "Sleep well, Quinn."

He slipped out and eased the door shut behind him. He stood in the hall until he heard the deadbolt snick shut. He jogged down the stairs. Thank heaven for soft bottomed dress shoes.

He looked up at her window. She stood in the window, backlit by the room lights. An angel watching over his departure. He smiled and waved. She waved and stepped back. The drapes swished shut and after a moment, the light went out. Almost immediately, the bedroom light snapped on.

He forced himself to drive away and not linger thinking about what was happening in her bedroom. He was not that guy. He was a decent respectful human. Most of the time.

The drive home, like every drive in Half Moon Bay, was short. He kicked off his shoes, hung his jacket and tie over a chair and flopped onto the couch. He checked his messages, set his alarm, and closed his eyes.

He was getting in too deep. Every moment with Quinn was a pleasure. A guilty treat. After the gift opening, he was walking away ... before it was too late.

After a fast shower and beard trim, Tyson headed for the inn. He couldn't wait for all the wedding shenanigans to be over with so he could get back to his normal routine. This was the second weekend in a row that he'd been distracted from his Find A Wife Plan. Also known as Evict Quinn from his Head. He was missing dating opportunities for all these wedding events.

The parking lot was nearly full. A double check of his watch revealed that he wasn't late. In fact, he was early. He was barely in the front door when his mother bustled over and grabbed him by the arm. She dragged him down the hall to a quiet spot.

"What are you doing?" she asked in *that* tone. The one that meant he'd messed something up.

"Coming to the gift opening?"

"Don't you be sassy. What were you thinking? Staying all night at Quinn's place? You have a reputation to uphold. You can't be sleeping around. Not if you want to become a school board administrator." she tsked. "Don't you boys ever think ahead?"

"What are you talking about? I did not spend the night with Quinn," he growled. His shoulders tensed up. "Who told you that?"

"Several people."

"Mom. I swear, I did not spend the night with Quinn Davidson."

"I saw your truck there myself."

What? What had she been doing out that late? He put the question into words. "I thought you went home right after the band shut down."

"Where I go and what I do is none of your business. I asked for an explanation."

She was frowning at him, but something wasn't adding up. For several weeks, she'd been pushing him toward Quinn. Just like she'd pushed his brothers toward their wives and fiancées. Now she was warning him off. What was up with that?

"I did not spend the night with Quinn. I. Did. Not. Sleep. With Her." He whispered each word as its own sentence. "Want to tell me what you were doing out so late that you thought I was there all night?" he prodded.

"No. Watch yourself. Mrs. Gilbert brought it up as well. She's on the school board. She'll vote you down if there's even a hint of a scandal around you. Pull yourself together. Find a woman. Get married. Stop all this messing around. I know you sneak off to the city every weekend for dates. Sooner or later, that'll come back to haunt you as well." She gave him another frown.

"I got a private message from Mrs. Jepsom today. It had a picture of you and Quinn in a hotel lobby. What's that all about?" Her tone said she had an idea and wasn't impressed.

Holy deflated footballs. The jerk from the hotel must have posted some security camera images. Not good.

"We were in the city running wedding errands for Heather and Zander. Ask him if you don't believe me. I was too tired to drive so we stayed over. That's it."

She gave him The Mom Look. "You better not be fibbing, young man. If you are, you'll regret it, especially if Mrs. Gilbert hears about it."

"Yes, ma'am." What else could he say? She was his mother. Like it or not, she was right, Mrs. Gilbert had more power than he wanted to admit.

His mother patted his cheek. "That's my boy. Now let's go to this party. Perhaps there's a nice local girl you could date."

As if he hadn't already checked out the local dating pool. Fishing was slim in Half Moon Bay dating waters. He didn't want a premade family, or a woman with a questionable past. He'd dated everyone else at one point or another. He needed chemistry. There had to be something special between him and his future wife if it was going to work. Something like the sparks he felt with Quinn. *Don't go there. Not in your head. Not in real life.*

Speaking of Quinn, where was she?

Chapter Thirteen

Quinn's stomach roiled, waking her before her alarm went off. She suffered through a series of dry heaves and struggled to the kitchen for some crackers. Surprisingly, her morning coffee didn't upset her stomach further.

Sitting at the table, head cradled in her hands, she admitted it was time to take the test. There was no real doubt that she was pregnant. She'd admitted that days ago. But a small part of her knew she needed to remove that last inkling of doubt and start planning.

She jumped up, half giddy. "I'm pregnant," she whispered. Hugging herself, she said it louder. She hopped around and shouted, "I'm pregnant." Laughing, she headed for the shower.

Her life was falling to bits. She had so many things to organize and plan and change. But she was ecstatic. She wanted a family. Just not yet. And not as a single mother. One thing she knew for sure ... the universe did not care about your plans. You had to adapt and roll with the punches.

She yawned her way through the shower, torn between elation and worry. First things first. It was early on Sunday morning. The churchgoers would be at church. The partiers would still be in bed. It was the best time to hit the drugstore for a test. She'd grab one on her way to the gift opening.

Oh, busted blisters. Her car was at the community center. She was going to have to rush if she planned to walk there and then get her test. Too bad she didn't have more time.

Only an early bird like Heather would plan an event at nine in the morning. It was part gift opening and part breakfast. Sammi, Tyson's brother Derrick's fiancée, was cooking breakfast for the inn, and the wedding goers. Heather was officially on her honeymoon or would be after breakfast.

She hadn't been to a gift opening before. She assumed it was casual. She hoped. She stood for way too long in front of her open closet doors, hand on her belly, trying to decide what to wear. Eventually, she settled on a pretty golden tunic dress, some thin brown tights, and her brown leather ankle boots.

Half an hour later, her stomach trembled as she stared at the drugstore's front door. It wasn't morning sickness this time. It was pure fear. Her phone beeped with a fifteen-minute warning. She'd have to move if she was going to get to the inn on time.

Inside, she piled a bunch of random items into a small basket. She searched the store for Mr. Edgar, he was nowhere in sight. She'd been hoping he'd be at the register. He usually was on Sunday mornings while his gossiping wife was at church. Today, a young woman was standing there, smacking her gum. Jenn was a former patient of Quinn's. During one of their sessions, Jenn had waxed poetic on how handsome the Bellamie brothers were and how she's like to snag herself one. Quinn ended that stream of conversation at once. She liked to get to know her patients, but not that personally.

Her phone beeped her next reminder. Well, she was out of time. She strode confidently to the register and dropped her pile on the counter. The pregnancy test was firmly buried under a gardening magazine, a bottle of water, two pairs of funky socks, three bags of candy, deodorant, toothpaste, a jar of antacids, earrings, and a hairbrush she didn't need. With any luck, Jenn wouldn't even notice the test among the pile.

She beeped the items through with a total lack of interest until she spied the box. She picked it up, looked at it, and looked at Quinn with a smirk.

Crap.

With luck, she'd be discreet. In the past, Mr. Edgar had fired people for gossiping about customer purchases. Hopefully Jenn would keep her mouth shut.

Quinn piled everything into her reuseable tote and strolled casually to her car. It was all she could do not to run, but that would only heighten Jenn's interest. Finally, she was safe inside her car. She opened the water and took a few cautious sips. Her mouth was Sahara dry, and she'd rather glug the water, but didn't want to risk a stomach upset.

She closed her eyes and leaned back against the seat, her heart pounding. Fear of discovery, fear of being pregnant and fear of being disappointed if she wasn't all battled for supremacy in her heart and brain. Why did life have to be so complicated?

She rested her hand on her belly. It was early, but she was almost certain it wasn't as flat as it had been two weeks ago. "Nonsense. It's much too early to see any changes. You're not quite four weeks," she reminded herself.

"We'll be fine," she whispered to her belly. "Won't we Little Bean?"

She yawned deeply. It was an unusually warm day for February fifteenth and the sun shone brightly into her vehicle making it toasty warm. She'd just sit here a moment and gather her equilibrium before she went to the inn. She had to be there. One of her tasks as maid of honor was to record the gifts and who gave them. She'd just sit a minute and then go.

Quinn jerked awake. "What?" she mumbled. It took twenty seconds for her to get her bearings. She was still in the drugstore parking lot. A dark shape loomed outside her window. She could barely see due to the sun behind it. A man's hand tapped on her window.

"Quinn? Are you okay?" He opened the door.

She turned toward him. "Tyson? What are you doing here?"

"Looking for you. You're late. You're not answering your phone. Heather asked me to check on you. I was on my way to your place when I saw your car. Are you okay?"

"I'm fine. I'll meet you at the inn."

"I don't think so. If you're tired enough to fall asleep in a parking lot, you are too tired to drive. I'll take you there myself."

"Tyson—"

"Quinn, don't fight me on this." He frowned. "I've got enough on my plate right now. Just lock up your car and get into my truck. Please." The please was a definite afterthought.

"But ... my car."

"We'll come back here later ... if you aren't so tired. Whatever happens, I'll make sure you get your car back safely. Okay?" The look on his face was pure impatience.

She was too tired to fight him. "Fine." She grabbed her wallet, beeped her car locks, and climbed into his truck. As they drove away, she saw Jenn standing in the drugstore window with a smug grin.

Oh, broken workout bands, this was not good.

Quinn sat silently on the ride to the inn.

"Are you okay?" Tyson asked as he pulled past the inn to the rear parking lot. "You're pale."

"I'm fine. A bit tired." She hurried to add, "But I really enjoyed myself last night. You are very pleasant company."

"You are as well." He didn't look at her, but he seemed to be hiding something.

"Are you okay?" She turned his earlier question back on him as he parked.

"I've got a lot on my mind. Let's get this done. I've had my fill of wedding related events. When I get married, it's a simple backyard ceremony with my family and a barbecue. No gifts. No fancy parties and dinners and practices. Short and sweet for me all the way." He snapped his mouth shut so hard his teeth clicked.

"I could go either way," she admitted honestly. "Fancy or simple. I just want to have a memorable day with my husband and his family. Maybe my closest friends."

He leaped out of the truck and rushed around to open her door. Obviously, the subject was closed. He offered her his hand and helped her down, though the truck wasn't that high.

"Thank you." She moved forward when he gestured for her to go ahead of him. "Thanks for coming to get me."

Heather rushed up to them as soon as they entered the back door. "There you are! I was getting worried about you." She wrapped Quinn in a warm hug and whispered, "Watch your back. Ty's mom is upset at you." She pulled back and clapped her hands together. "Let's do this. I've got a plane to catch. Hawaii awaits. I can't wait to soak up some sun beside my husband. Everyone is waiting for us. Come on."

The gift opening was a lot more fun than Quinn expected. Even Tyson laughed at some of the joke gifts that were hidden among the actual presents. People came and went as Zander and Heather worked their way through the large pile. There were quiet side conversations and servers strolling through, occasionally refilling coffee and tea and clearing plates.

They finished everything up and Quinn closed the pretty floral notebook she'd recorded everything in. She tucked it inside a gift bag with the cards and handed Zander the checks, cash, and gift cards that had been given.

He tucked them into his wallet and taking Heather by the hand declared, "Thank you all for coming, and for the amazing presents. When I figure out who gave us that box of adult diapers, I'll get even." The crowd laughed just as hard at his taunt as they had at the joke gift. "Now, if you'll forgive us, Heather and I have a plane to catch. We'll see you all in two weeks."

"Thank you everyone," Heather called as Zander led her toward the front door.

The crowd milled around making small talk. Tyson's mother, Beth strode toward Quinn, a look of determination on her face. "Quinn, can you help me carry some of these gifts to the guest house out back? Tyson's brother Jacob lived in the small house behind the larger inn.

They gathered up a few things and before Quinn could figure out why there was such a rush to move the gifts, Beth had her cornered in the guest house.

"Quinn, are you pregnant?" She asked the second the door closed behind them.

"Um. What?"

"It's a simple question, really. Are you pregnant?" She repeated the words slowly as if she thought doing so would make them easier to understand.

"First, I don't believe that is any of your business."

"Of course it is," she interrupted. "You've been spending a lot of time with my son. He has a reputation to uphold. Is it Tyson's child? Are you carrying my grandchild?" Her voice was hopeful.

Which was it? Did she need Quinn to stay away from Tyson, or did she want a grandchild?

"I have never slept with your son. Not that it's any of your business." She almost winced at the rude words.

"I have seen pictures of you checking into a hotel." Her voice was pure accusation.

"On an errand for the inn and the wedding. Nothing personal."
That danged desk clerk and his nose for gossip.

The door opened and Tyson strode in his arms burdened by bulging gift bags. "Ladies, you're blocking the doorway. Scoot in, please."

Quinn wiped her feet and carried her pile of gifts further into the house.

"It's good that you're both here," Beth said as she set her own stack of gifts on the kitchen table.

"Why's that?" Tyson asked.

Quinn sucked in a breath and swallowed her rising nausea. She inched toward the door but Beth jumped in front of her with the speed and agility of a cat.

"Not so fast, young lady."

Shocked, Quinn halted in her tracks. She stopped so quickly she nearly tipped over. If Tyson hadn't been there, she'd have hit the floor. That mom voice was intimidating. She stood there blinking.

"Mom, let it go."

"Let what go?" she said at the exact moment his mother said, "I will not!"

"You don't know what you're talking about, and I promise you, you are wrong." Warning darkened his voice.

"Tyson Christopher Bellamie, you will hear me out."

"Mo-om. No." Definitely angry.

"Mrs. Bellamie, I'm not sure what you think is going on, but I'd like to leave now. Please and thank you."

"Young lady, you hold on one danged minute. Tyson, zip it." She planted her hands on her hips hard enough that her gray hair bounced. "Not one single word out of either of you until I say my piece."

"Mo-"

"I said zip." She glared from Tyson to Quinn and back. Twice. "Let's start with the rumors. One, you are seeing each other behind my back. Two, Tyson is dating hundreds of women in the city. Three, Quinn has been ill. Four, Quinn bought a pregnancy kit. Five, you spent the night together last night. Now, you first Quinn. Which of these are true?"

"Um. Not meaning to be rude, but I don't see how my life is any of your business, Mrs. Bellamie."

"My son has career plans. It seems his dating life is going to kill those aspirations. I want to clear things up. If you are dating, fine. If you are pregnant, yahoo, but if you are, my son will do right by you." Her voice was calmer than the words implied.

Mortification swamped her. How could this woman, this virtual stranger think she had any control over Quinn's life? What happened between her and Tyson, not that there was anything, was none of her danged business.

Broken shoelaces, she wanted to cuss this woman out. She was infuriating. This was humiliating, even if her meddling may have been meant with an odd sort of kindness.

"Any child I might or might not be carrying has nothing to do with your son. I have never slept with your son. As you probably know, I just left a long-term relationship."

Tyson interrupted. "Every moment I spent with Quinn was either with her as my physiotherapist or wedding related. We don't associate for any other reason. Mom, there is nothing between us."

A bit of Quinn's heart dried up and crumbled off. Her chest was tight, and tears burned in the back of her eyes. Wow. She'd thought, okay hoped, they'd been forming at least a friendship, maybe more. Her anger soared. "I'll thank you to mind your own business, Mrs. Bellamie."

Yikes, she hadn't just said that, had she? She was as hormonal as a rabbit in the spring. Not good.

"Mom. Leave it."

"Look you two. You are great kids. Quinn, either stay away from my son or marry him before more people learn about your pregnancy. I will not stand for you ruining his reputation and hurting his career." She turned to Tyson who was white with shock. "Tyson, do the right thing." Her voice held both hope and censure.

She dusted her hands together. "Now, I'll just leave you two to talk."

Quinn stared at the door as it closed without a sound. Her heart pounded and her knees became weak. She trembled all over with a heart-sick chill. She hadn't wanted Tyson to know about the baby. Not until she had a solid plan. She staggered into the living room and flopped on the couch, head in hands. Nausea washed over her, and she gagged.

"Are you okay?" Tyson asked. "Can I get you anything?"

"Water. Saltines. Please."

He padded away, his sock feet not making any noise on the hardwood floor. He was back in seconds. "Here you go."

She took the cool glass in her hand and sipped. He sat beside her on the couch, close but not touching. "Is it true?"

"No. Yes. Maybe." She nibbled another cracker. "Probably. I haven't taken the test yet." She looked at him, hoping her tears didn't show. "This isn't your problem. Rest assured, I know who the father is, and I can handle this on my own. I'll make sure the world knows that this is not your child. I won't ruin your reputation."

She had no idea how she'd manage that, but she'd find a way, even if it meant moving away and making a fresh start somewhere else.

Gah! This was all ridiculous. This wasn't the Victorian age. Woman had babies alone every day. Thousands of them. Some by choice, some by accident, some through tragedy. There was no stigma in being an unwed mother. The idea was archaic.

Unfortunately, Half Moon Bay was a small town, and the Bellamie family had a sterling reputation to maintain. She didn't want to make his life miserable. She liked Tyson. Heck, she probably loved him. For certain she enjoyed his company and his kind heart.

"Maybe you should take that test," he suggested. "Do you have one?"

"I do." She snorted to herself. How much she wished those two words meant something else between them. "I'll take it when I get home." She rose to her feet.

"I'll take you back to your car. We can go to your place and take the test."

"You're kidding right?"

"What?" He looked confused.

"We were just read the riot act by your mother. You can't spend another second around me. Your reputation will be ruined. I can't let that happen. No sense destroying both our lives."

"Is that what you think?" he snapped. "That this baby will destroy your life? Children are a blessing."

"Don't take my words out of context." She stabbed him in the chest with her finger. "I love my child already. But I will not let my child ruin your life, your career. Walk away Tyson. Walk away."

"Quinn you're too upset to drive."

"Well, I'm sure not taking a ride home from you." She jumped up. "I'll take an Uber."

"There isn't one in Half Moon Bay."

"Fine. A taxi. Whatever. I'll walk. It's not far."

"You are upset, you're exhausted, you've got bags under your eyes."

"Gee, thanks. Kick me when I'm down, why don't ya?" She was picking a fight now. She knew he meant the comment sympathetically.

He pushed out a harsh breath. "Quinn, please may I drive you home? I'll get Derrick or Jacob to bring you your car."

"Fine." She was too exhausted—emotionally, and physically—to argue any longer. She just wanted to curl up and cry. Nothing like a hormone-driven pity party to make things better.

Chapter Fourteen

Tyson looked at Quinn as he drove the short distance to her apartment building. She had purplish bruised-looking bags under her eyes. They hadn't been there earlier, so they must be the result of her exhaustion. He'd worked with enough pregnant teachers to understand how draining pregnancy could be. He wanted to tuck her in and make sure she got some rest.

Dang his mother. What was she thinking attacking Quinn like that? He'd have a word with her later. After he got Quinn home and found a way to cool his anger at his mother. For Quinn, he felt nothing but sympathy.

Liar. You care for her and want to help her.

He hushed the voice whispering in his head. He'd stand by her while she took the test. Then, they'd go their separate ways, despite what his mother said. He pulled up in front of her building and she hopped out almost before the truck stopped.

"Thanks for the ride. Catch you later."

He shut the truck off and hopped out. "Let me walk you upstairs. You're exhausted."

"Tyson, people might be watching. If you leave me here, they'll assume it is wedding related. If you come up, they'll have doubts. Let's not make this worse."

He debated listening to her. No doubt she was right. But something in him wouldn't do that to her. She was weak and upset. She needed a friend, and he'd be that friend since her bestie was on her honeymoon.

"Let them think whatever the hell they like," he snapped. "You need a friend right now. I'm here. I'll walk you up."

He took her by the elbow and led her inside. Her protest was weak and short lived. She moved slowly up the stairs. He stuck close to her side, one step lower, in case she tumbled. It would be tragic if something happened to her or her baby.

His mind churned and roiled. It was like a lightning storm in his head. Flashes of thoughts and unformed ideas. Thunderous voices speaking all at once and falling into aching silence that confused him and made his head ache.

He'd love to blame his aching head on booze. Not that he was a big drinker. He rarely drank except on Zander's deck in the evening. He was stone-cold sober yesterday, last night, and today. Yet he felt like he had a five-alarm hangover. Pounding head, racing heart, upset stomach, unformed anxiety.

He tried to logic it out as they crept up the stairs. He was worried about what his mom thought of him. What son wouldn't be? He was worried about his job and his reputation. Again, who wouldn't be?

He could get another job. There were other schools. There were other careers. He got calls to coach at least once a month and three sports networks were hounding him to be a sportscaster. The only concern left ...

He stopped on the final landing.

That left Quinn and the baby. He was worried about them. Deeply worried. About their health and their future. How would Quinn manage as a single mother? What was childcare like? What did it cost? How could she recover from birth if she had to go straight back to work?

Who was the father?

It had to be Duke.

Had she told him? Was she going to?

Too many questions, all tangled up in a ball of anxiety and trepidation.

She stood in the open doorway to her hall and stared at him. "Are you coming? Or did you change your mind?"

The fear in her voice galvanized him into action. "Come on." He took her by the elbow and led her down the hall. "Let's get you inside and put your feet up. I'll make you some tea."

"I'd kill for coffee," she muttered and unlocked the door.

He helped her out of her jacket, shed his, and hung them up. "Are you allowed coffee?" he asked.

"Maybe? That is, I think I can have some. I just can't overdo it. Maybe one cup." She headed into the kitchen.

"Let me get it. I know how to make coffee."

"First cupboard on top, right above the brewer," she said before he could look for what he needed. He liked how she seemed to anticipate his questions. She'd done it before. "I've got this. Why don't you go rest? How do you like it?"

"One cream, one sugar," she said. "Thanks."

She padded past him, and he heard her settle herself. Hopefully the couch where she could stretch out and relax. He stared at the brown brew as it dripped slowly into the pot. With each second that passed, the pot grew fuller and his emotions calmer.

There was an idea blooming in the back of his mind.

He knew the feeling from his football days. Back then, he'd get an idea for a play, but it would come to him slowly. First the inkling that something was there. Then a hint, then a full-blown play.

It was that way for Christmas gifts too. Absolutely no idea, then the certainty that he'd find the perfect gift. Then the gift itself. His mind worked in layers. He'd embraced that years ago. More than once it had come in handy dealing with students and their families.

It happened like that when he realized the school janitor, Harry Webb, needed to retire. One step at a time the plan had come to him. Then, he executed it the same way. Give Harry an assistant. Then an extra day off here and there. Harry had lost his wife. Work was all he had, and Tyson hated to retire him. In the end, the elderly gentleman started taking more time off for one thing or another. As he was paid hourly, it was no loss to the school if he didn't show up. Last week, Harry came into the office and put in his notice. He'd been spending his days off at the seniors' center playing cards and shuffleboard. He wanted more time to do that.

Tyson pulled down some mugs and poured the coffee. As he stirred cream and sugar into them both, his mind focused on Quinn and what he could do to help her. For now, he'd make sure her immediate needs were taken care of. Later, when his idea finished forming, he'd put it into action.

He poked at his mind, impatient to know what the plan was, because right now, at this moment, he had no idea what he could do for her. It would bloom to fruition in its own time, but impatience pushed at him.

He carried the cups to the living room. Quinn was curled up on the couch on her side. A red and gold crochet blanket covered her up to her chin. Hands under her cheek, she rested on a matching pillow. Sound asleep. Perfect. She needed the rest.

He sat down after putting her coffee on a coaster. No sense in waking her up for coffee. He'd hang around and make sure she got something to eat before he left. Mornings were often tough on pregnant women and two of his teachers had turned ravenous as soon as their morning sickness wore off. Quinn had not eaten at the inn. He'd been unable to stop watching her. She'd need food when she woke. Come to think of it, he hadn't eaten either. His appetite had vanished when his mom confronted him. It had been resurfacing when she cornered him with Quinn. It was gone now.

That brought up another issue. What could he do about his mom?

He drank four cups of coffee while he waited for Quinn to wake up. He probably could have gone home. He debated it more than once. In the end, he couldn't make himself leave.

The door buzzer rang. He jumped up to answer it.

"Hello."

"It's Derrick. I've got the keys and the bag she left in the car."

Ty buzzed him in. Derrick had a date with Sammi, so he didn't hang around. Tyson returned to the living room and set the bag on the table. Quinn sat up and rubbed her eyes.

"How long was I asleep?" she mumbled and ran her hands over her hair, flattening the bits that stuck up.

"Two hours, give or take. Derrick brought your keys, and your bag." He pointed to the coffee table. "Do you want coffee? How about lunch?"

"Food would be amazing. But I'll get it."

"Relax. I'll order something. What do you feel like? Jimmy's Pancake House makes the best waffles."

"Wouldn't they get cold on the way here?"

"I just pop them in the toaster and they're just like fresh. With bacon and some of their mixed fruit topping, it's a reasonably healthy way to fill the belly." He looked at her, giving her sleepy brain a moment to process.

"Make it sausages and you've got a deal. No, wait. Bacon and sausages. Waffles, and scrambled eggs. I'm ravenous."

He laughed. "I thought you might be." He called the order in and made fresh coffee. Decaf. She'd never know, and he wouldn't have to regret the extra caffeine intake. He was vibrating enough already.

He carried the refilled cups to the living room. "Here you go." She sat back, cup in hand. She looked better without the dark bags under her eyes. He wondered when the last time was that she'd gotten a good night's rest. "Maybe you should take the test."

"I'm scared," she admitted without looking at him.

"Isn't it better to know, than to delay and worry? I've read that babies can sense extra strong emotions."

"When did you read that?" she asked.

While you were asleep, however, he wasn't about to share that snippet of information. "I don't recall exactly." *Somewhere between article two and seventeen.* "Take the test, knowing one way or another will relieve some of the stress."

"Or add more." She pulled a long thin box from the bag Derrick had brought. "It'll add more worries if it is positive."

"Will it? Really? You're a smart woman. I'd wager that you are already calculating costs, fixing plans, and organizing things in your mind. Those worries might remain, or they'll vanish if the test is negative."

"You're right."

She didn't sound at all certain, but she took the test to the bathroom and left him there waiting. Worrying.

Chapter Fifteen

Quinn stared at the plus sign on the strip of plastic she had in her hand. She compared it to the first one. Both tests said the same thing. She was pregnant.

She exhaled and drew in a shaky breath.

Tension slid from her shoulders and landed in her tummy.

"Shoot. Broken shoelaces. Twisted sports tape," she muttered her curse replacements to herself.

She looked at the tests again and dropped, weak-kneed, onto the toilet. The lid was up, and she nearly fell in. Overcome with laughter, she dropped to her knees on the floor, arms wrapped around her middle.

She was having a baby.

SHE WAS HAVING A BABY!

Tyson knocked on the door. "Quinn? Quinn? Are you okay in there?"

She gasped, trying to stop her silent laugher. She tried to say she was fine, but it came out garbled.

"I'm coming in," Ty warned. He knocked again and the door slowly opened.

He fell to his knees beside her. "Are you okay?" he demanded. "Do you need a doctor. Oh, God, is it a miscarriage?" He stroked her back and tried to ease her hair back out of her face.

She laughed harder and tears streamed down her face.

"I'll call 911."

"Don't," she gasped. "I ... I ... I'm good."

He helped her sit up; his hands warm on her shoulders. She hadn't turned up the heat when she got home and she was chilled right through, though possibly, some of her chill was from the two positive test sticks.

"What is it? Are you pregnant?"

Unable to speak past the lump in her throat, she nodded and swallowed. "I am."

"Congratulations. You'll be a good mom. Let me help you to the couch. You don't want to stay here on the floor. You'll catch a chill."

She trembled as he helped her stand. Her knees were shaking, and her teeth chattered. She was excited and so scared she wanted to barf.

"I made more coffee. It'll warm you up. Come on now. Let's get you seated." He led her to the couch and helped her sit. He draped an afghan over her lap and another around her shoulders. Then he pressed her blessedly warm mug in her hands and guided it to her mouth. "Drink up."

"Wait. I shouldn't? Should I?"

"One cup per day according to the internet. But this is decaf. It'll be fine."

He'd been reading about pregnancy when she was asleep. Who was this man? He'd shown more care and concern today than Duke ever had, even if you combined every nice thing Duke had done for her since she'd known him.

"Thank you," she whispered. Her voice would crack if she tried to speak aloud. He helped her take small sips. "I'm okay now."

He moved from being perched on the edge of the coffee table to sit beside her. "Are you sure?"

"I mean, I'm back in control. I'm scared. I'm excited. Oh my gosh, I have so much to do. I have to make a list, so I don't forget anything." She started pushing the blankets off. She needed a pen and paper.

"Whoa there, momma. Take it easy. You've got months to make plans."

"I guess so." She covered herself up again. "I'm excited."

"And scared no doubt. Have you told the father?"

"No. And don't you tell him either." She leaned forward in tune with her passionate response. "He's a liar and a cheater. The day I dumped him, he made it clear that he was just using me." Her cheeks heated. She was still mortified that she hadn't realized that while she was in a relationship, Duke was just using her as a hookup. "I don't want that type of influence in my child's life. I might not know where I'm going, or what I'm doing. I've got a lot to learn about pregnancy, babies, and parenting. But the one thing I know for certain is that Duke will never know about this child. He probably wouldn't believe me anyway."

She leaned back again. "I've got this." *I think. No, I'll do what needs done for me and my baby. I do have this.* Her silent cheerleader kicked in with the voice of a confident optimist. "Anyway. I'm good now. You don't have to stay."

"Of course I do. I ordered lunch. It should be here any minute." He shifted positions until his back was in the corner of the sofa and he was facing her.

His steady regard was unnerving.

"Oh, right. I forgot," she blurted. She tried not to stare at him. But Lord help her, he was lovely. Handsome, kind, understanding, and obviously not judging her for getting pregnant. He'd stuck up for her with his mother. Just look at him there, making sure she was okay. Feeding her and bringing her coffee. Her heart cracked a little. After they ate, he'd leave, and their short nearly-a-relationship would be over.

Apparently, there were already rumors about them, but she would cut those off immediately. She'd tell everyone she had a boyfriend out of town. If she had to, she'd hire an actor to play her boyfriend to protect Tyson's reputation.

She hated that reputation. So important to him and his mother.

Still, he'd never made her feel unworthy.

Though obviously, he thought she was, or they would have pursued this attraction between them instead of ignoring it. He'd never said anything, but she was one hundred percent certain that he felt it too. She'd caught him sneaking looks at her.

They shared several interests and had the same sense of humor. He knew almost as much about *Star Trek* as she did. They were completely compatible. Except for his stupid reputation. It had come up over and over, and not once had he said why she wasn't suitable. She was half tempted to ask. If she wasn't so emotionally wrung out already, she'd ask.

The question bubbled just behind her lips until it burst out. "Ty? I have a question."

The door buzzer chimed.

Aargh. Busted heating packs.

Saved by the bell. Or was that diverted?

She fumed about the interruption until Ty asked her to come to the table to eat. She didn't want to move from her cozy spot, but she joined him at the table. They ate in near silence, the only discussion revolving around the amazingly delicious breakfast.

"Come on, I'll tuck you back in. You probably want a nap."

"I'm fine." Her yawn called her a liar.

"I don't think you are. Let's get you comfortable, then I'll clean up the kitchen."

"You should just go. Your truck's been outside for way too long. People will talk." She didn't care but knew that he did.

She stomped to the couch and lay down, deliberately taking up the entire length to ensure he had no room. Not that he was likely to stay.

"You started to ask me a question earlier. What was on your mind?" He lay the soft afghan over her body and started to tuck her in.

"Leave. I can cover myself." She didn't mean to snap at him, but he was killing her with kindness, and she couldn't take it for another second.

He jumped back. "Whoa." He stared down at her, his brown eyes confused. He scratched his beard. "Is that how you treat a friend?"

She jerked upright. "Is that what we are? Friends?"

"What does that mean?" He paused, obviously confused. "Of course we're friends. My brother just married your best friend. We'll see each other all the time. That makes us friends. Practically family."

"What's wrong with me, Tyson? Why aren't I good enough for you?" She stood up and paced to the window and back. "You drive hundreds of miles every weekend to meet up with women you meet on the internet. But I'm right here!" She trembled with fury. "I'm right in front of you."

She jabbed him in the chest. "I like you. A lot. Too much. We get along. We share a dozen common interests. We have the same values. But you won't even look at me most of the time. But here you are, in my apartment being all kind and solicitous. Almost like you cared, but I swear to God that you wouldn't date me if I was the last woman on earth. Why, Tyson? Why?"

She couldn't stand to look at the panic and confusion on his face. She stormed over to the window and stared out at the street. Light snow drifted down melting on impact with the pavement. It lingered on the grass in the park across the street. The roads would be messy tomorrow. But not as messy as this disaster of a friendship.

She hated Tyson Bellamie, too much to put into words.

Jerk.

Stupid Tyson Jerk-Face.

Chapter Sixteen

O *h no!* He should have known this was coming.

The urge to bolt and leave her hanging was strong. He clenched his fists and curled his toes into the throw rug. His chest hurt where she jabbed him. If she'd hit him, she would have knocked him on his butt.

Weak winter daylight streamed through the window, backlighting her in an echo of seeing her looking down on him last night. He'd been touched that she watched him leave. She was a nice woman, and if not for her past of dating a ton of men and her on-again off-again relationship with Duke, she'd make a good wife.

He'd had this argument with his mother and his brother Zander. Neither could understand why Quinn wasn't right for him. Nobody got it. He'd thought for a moment yesterday that his mother understood. But she'd been playing him. She wanted to trap them into a marriage so she could have more grandkids.

He fumbled for a way to explain himself. One that wouldn't hurt her feelings more than they already were. He didn't want to date or marry her, but he didn't want to hurt her unnecessarily either.

"Why, Tyson?" she repeated.

He blew out a breath that did nothing to calm the roiling in his stomach.

"Don't I deserve an answer? Don't I deserve to know why you hang around, but won't date me? Lord knows I've hinted enough that I'm interested. I've practically begged you. If I thought dropping my clothing and seducing you would work, I'd have tried that."

When she turned from the window, her glare would have melted the polar ice caps. "You know what? Never mind. Screw you Tyson Pristine Reputation Bellamie. I'm more than good enough for you. I'm too good for you. Get the hell out of my apartment and don't ever come back. Don't speak to me. Don't think about me. Don't talk to me. Consider yourself shunned. Evicted. A persona non-grata."

"Don't I get a chance to explain myself?"

"I'd like you to leave."

"Not before I've said my piece."

Her eyes rolled so hard it made his hurt. She made a go-ahead gesture and crossed her arms over her chest.

"You're a nice woman," he started.

"Ya, I know that" she interrupted.

"Are you going to let me talk?" Did she have to make this harder? He was struggling as it was.

She mimed zipping her lips and her expression was one hundred percent sarcasm. He almost laughed. He admired her spunk.

"I have plans. Big plans. I want to be an administrator for the school board. I'd like to work my way up to the state level. There are changes that could be made to immensely improve school life for high school students. My students. I want the best for them."

Her expression soured more than it already was. Her brows pinched together, and the corners of her mouth turned down. She looked like she'd just sucked a lemon. Not good.

"Many of the board members are ... how should I say it? Stuffy. They have values that are decades behind the times. They're judgmental and critical. I cannot risk my life going against their values. It could cost me my dream job."

Her shoulders hunched up as if he'd hit her. Her cheeks were glowing red, and her fists were clenched with the effort to keep quiet. She nodded as if to say, 'go on'.

"I'm looking for a woman with a clean reputation. Honestly, Quinn. I like you. A lot. If I was another man, I'd want to pursue a relationship with you. Take the next step and start dating to see where it went. But I'm not that guy. It isn't nice but dating you would put me on the board's radar because when you first got to Half Moon Bay, you dated. A lot. Then there's the whole Duke thing. Your on-and-off relationship with him paints you in a bad light. He's a loser. He can't keep a job. He drinks and drives. You are guilty by association." He winced. Even to himself his words sounded ridiculous.

"And you don't think your precious board is going to get wind of you dating hundreds of women a year? How will they judge that?

Will they think you're looking for a wife? Or will they assume you're having random hookups?"

He hadn't thought of that. It didn't matter. He was discreet. Nobody knew.

Quinn knew, his mind whispered.

Zander knew. He must have heard it from Heather. No doubt Zander shared everything with his new wife. But they were family, and they'd never share his dating habits publicly.

"Nobody knows what I do in my free time."

"And yet your mother called you on it today. She knows about your dating habits. That'll get back to the board. Secrets always come out. Always."

"I'll be engaged by then. It won't matter." At least he hoped that was the case. "For now, and always, I'll keep my reputation intact."

"You don't think they know about all the women you dated during your football career? How many were there? Hundreds? I've seen the pictures online."

She'd looked him up online. Was that flattering, or creepy?

"I've already told you. I dated exactly two women during my career. The rest of them, the ones in the pictures wanted to date me. They were caught up in my fame, or the money they thought I had."

"And will the precious board know that?" She spat.

"They hired me. So, it must not matter to them. As long as I keep my nose clean now. I'm good. I will find a nice woman with a good reputation and marry her, then I'll get my dream job."

"I get it," she snapped. "You don't have the balls to go for what you want. I take it all back. I don't want you. I want a man, not a scared little boy who lives his life to please others and can't find the courage to live the life he wants."

She jabbed her hand toward the door. "Take your cowardly self and get out of my house. Don't come back. Ever. You aren't worth one more second of my time."

"Quinn ..." Her dismissal hurt. He didn't want her to be angry with him. Though they couldn't be friends anymore, he still wanted their relationship to be pleasant.

"Don't Quinn me. You don't want me? Well, Tyson, I don't want you either. We're all good." She stomped her foot.

There was no reasoning with her. Not in this mood.

"Goodbye, Quinn. It was nice knowing you. I'll see you around."

"Not if I see you first," she shouted at his back as he walked away.

He put his shoes on, grabbed his jacket and left. He should have been relieved.

Why wasn't he?

Why did it feel like he'd lost something, someone, valuable?

He rubbed the ache in his chest and trudged down the stairs. He couldn't help but look up at her window. Her painfully empty window.

Chapter Seventeen

M onday morning came way too quickly. Quinn wanted to hide in her bed and ignore the world. Instead, she pasted on her best smile and headed for the hospital. She had a long list of patients today. Her schedule was booked solid, plus she was on call if the emergency room needed anyone to give advice to injured patients. Just what she needed. She walked the short distance, careful not to slip on the bits of ice that lay everywhere after yesterday's snowfall.

The hospital was a modern three-story building, and her department was on the third floor. She trudged up the steps. Behind her, someone jogged up them.

"Morning, Quinn," Jeff Trask greeted her. They worked together for more days than not. The department had a rotating schedule for some of their casual employees. While Quinn worked days, Monday to Friday, Jeff worked ten days on and four days off. Most days you never knew who you were working with. She enjoyed working with Jeff, as he was usually quiet and kept to himself.

"Morning," she opened the final door and exited onto the third floor. "Nice day, isn't it."

"Beautiful," he enthused.

"You sound upbeat." Unlike herself who was still wallowing in misery after yesterday's debacle. She never should have pushed Tyson about their non-relationship.

"I am. I met someone this weekend. She works at Anchors Aweigh She's new in town. She's a server and she's amazing."

"I think I met her last week. Short blonde hair, brown eyes. About five-five?"

"That's my Allison. She's fabulous. We're meeting for lunch to-day." His grin was blinding. And annoying. She strode down the hall to their offices.

"Congrats. I hope it goes well for you."

"Thanks. And congrats to you too."

"What?" She stopped dead. How had he heard she was pregnant? Not good.

"Congrats. I hear you've been dating Tyson Bellamie. He's quite a catch. Heck of a football player, and a great administrator according to my sister. She's got kids in Tyson's school."

"Ty's a nice guy, but we're not dating."

"But you're always together, I assumed ..."

"His brother married my best friend. We were together a lot helping with wedding stuff. That's all." She barely got the words out through gritted teeth. She had to dispel this rumor fast. Before it got around.

She might hate Tyson, but she didn't want to hurt his reputation, even if she thought his insistence on keeping it to old school standards was ridiculous. She did not want people thinking she was carrying his baby.

"That's too bad. He's way better than that other guy you were dating."

"Why does everyone care who I'm dating?" she snapped, finally losing her cool. "It's nobody's business except mine."

Jeff jumped back and threw up his hands in a surrendering gesture. "Sorry. I'll drop it and mind my own business."

She sighed. "Sorry, Jeff. The wedding stuff took a lot out of me. I need more sleep."

"How about if I get you some tea? You like mint, right? You can chill before your first appointment arrives."

"Thanks, Jeff. Sorry I snapped at you."

"No worries. I'll be back in a flash with that tea." He turned and left the department. He must be going to the cafeteria instead of making tea in their tiny break room. Whatever. She was just glad to be alone.

Work kept her too busy to think about anything, save the occasional upset in her stomach which brought her situation home with the speed and impact of a runaway freight train.

One day passed and then another. First-trimester exhaustion helped her sleep, but her mornings and evenings were filled with longing and regrets. Maybe, if she'd kept her mouth shut, she wouldn't have pushed Tyson completely away. A bit of him was better than none of him.

She was trying not to harbor her regret. Dwelling on it wouldn't change her past. But she could be more cautious moving forward.

She tried. And tried. And failed to accept her mistake.

How could she escape it when the Bellamie name was everywhere? She walked past Bellamie High School every day. Tyson's truck sat in his parking stall, taunting her. The Bellamie curling rink. the Bellamie skating rink. Bellamie freaking everything.

She'd run into Beth in the grocery store. His brother, Derrick, at the hardware store, and his niece Ella at the library. There was literally no avoiding them. The only plus about the Bellamies was that her best friend, Heather, who was now a Bellamie, was due home from her honeymoon tomorrow. She couldn't wait to hear all about her friend's trip. She was so happy for Heather and Zander.

As she splashed through puddles on her way home, she considered moving away from Bellamieland. She could go back to Seattle or apply for a position in Anchorage. She had enjoyed living there, except for the ridiculously long winter. A seaside town would be best. She loved the ocean. Someplace small. Under about eight thousand would be great.

She wasn't going to be able to start her own business now that money was earmarked to keep her alive during her time off with Little Bean. Right. The baby. If she left, she'd likely lose her maternity leave. She'd have to stick it out until after the baby was born. She could do that. She'd survive this. You could live through anything if there was an end in sight.

Her phone vibrated in the pocket of the yoga pants she wore to work. She found it easier to demonstrate techniques in the snug pants than in the scrubs Jeff wore, or the dressier pants her female colleagues preferred. She was nearly home. Only a block to go. The message could wait.

She made herself a cup of chamomile tea, put a tray of cabbage rolls in the oven to heat, and sat down on the sofa to work on her needs versus wants list. There were a million things she should have. Some were necessities, some were luxuries. She'd be getting a new crib and car seat for sure, but she'd probably get a stroller second-hand. Same with a change table–dresser combination.

Her phone chimed again.

Right. Pregnancy brain. She'd forgotten to check her messages when she got home. She checked the display. Heather!

Heather: Can you come to dinner tomorrow?

Quinn: You're back? Already?

Heather: Yep. Came in last night. I miss you. Dinner's at six at our house.

Quinn: I'll be there.

Something to look forward to. She'd have to tell Heather about the baby. Soon. Not tonight. She wouldn't ruin her bestie's home-coming.

Waiting for dinner passed interminably. Work seemed to drag on and on and on. Patients were grumpy and disappointed in their progress. Little Bean was giving her an upset stomach all day. She ate two sleeves of saltines in secret. She wasn't ready to share her news with the world. Finally, she was at home. She took a quick shower and loaded up the cookies she'd grabbed at the bakery on her way home.

Heather and Zander lived outside of town in a large suite above Zander's veterinary clinic. They had an enormous yard with stables and pens for housing recuperating animals. Zander had a gift with wild critters and often rehabbed them for the local fish and wildlife department.

Today, the pens were empty, and the flower gardens bare. She didn't know how much gardening Zander had done in the past, but Heather had mentioned wanting to plant flowers this year. Quinn envied their domestic bliss.

She walked up the outside staircase to the suite and rapped on the door.

Inside, Heather squealed, "She's here!" The door flew open and before Quinn could say anything, she was in Heather's arms. "Oh, I missed you so much."

"Shut it. You did not. You were on your honeymoon." They laughed together and she took a moment to enjoy Heather's warmth and floral scent.

"Come in. Dinner's almost ready. I'm making chicken cordon bleu, rice pilaf, and baked butternut squash." She grabbed Quinn by the hand and dragged her inside. "Let me get your coat."

"I brought cookies." She was overwhelmed by the enthusiastic response. They were close friends; they'd been roommates but had known each other for less than a year. Heather needed a place to stay when she was hired by the inn, and Quinn needed a roommate. It was a match made in heaven. They'd ended up really hitting it off and their friendship had developed quickly.

"Hey, Quinn," Zander greeted her. "Can I get you something to drink? A glass of wine? A beer?"

"I'd love a ginger ale if you have one. If not, maybe a cup of tea."

Heather gave her a side glance and raised her left eyebrow.

"I'm tired. I haven't been sleeping well. I don't want to be sleepy, or wine-muddled for the drive home." One look at her friend showed she wasn't buying the explanation, but she let it go without comment.

"Ginger ale it is," Zander said, totally oblivious to the silent side conversation.

"Tell me about Hawaii. Was it beautiful? Hot? Amazing? I want all the details."

"It was hot," Zander mock grumbled. "Too much sand."

"Oh, hush." Heather swatted him on the shoulder. "It was amazing, and we had so much fun. Snorkeling was incredible. We rented a Go-Cam and we took the best pictures. I'm making an album as soon as I get the prints back."

"Volcanoes State Park was interesting. And when we visited Pearl Harbor, your friend was all teary-eyed. We toured the USS Arizona, which was fascinating," Zander added his input.

They sat at the table chatting about everything they'd seen and done while on their honeymoon. Quinn was fascinated, and admittedly a bit jealous of their fun.

"It sounds like you had a great time. I'd love to go some time."

"Oh," Heather jumped up. "I almost forgot. I got you something." She rushed out and came back with a woven beach bag and set it on the table. "The bag's yours, but the gift is inside."

The bag was pretty. Woven of pink natural fabric, it was painted with bright hibiscus flowers. "It's beautiful."

"It's made from leaves. It's called lauhala weaving. I got one for myself too. Open it."

"You didn't need to get me anything. But thank you. I love it." She opened the bag and peeked inside. A towel? She pulled the item out. It was a deep purple bath sheet printed with white flowers. It had to be four feet by six feet. It was enormous. "Wow. It's huge." She laughed with delight. "I love it."

"I have one too. We can sunbathe at the beach with them. Though it won't be quite the same as Hawaii." She chuckled. "Dig deeper."

The bag held two floral sundresses. They were a floaty and loose-fitting style. They'd be perfect to cover her baby bump this summer. It also held a pair of dangly shell and pearl earrings. Quinn gasped. They were exquisite. "Wow. Thank you so much. I can't wait to wear them."

"Try them on," Heather suggested. "I cleaned them when we got back. I want to see you wear them."

"Wear what?" Tyson strode into the kitchen.

Quinn's stomach dropped to her toes, and she wanted to disappear someplace far away. She didn't look at him, though her heart longed to.

"Tyson, bro. You made it." Zander got up and gave his brother a man hug and smacked him on the back a couple times. "Good to see you."

"Thanks for inviting me. Hi, Quinn."

"Tyson," she greeted him expressionlessly. Keep cool, Quinn. You can get through this. What was he doing here?

"What are we trying on?" Tyson asked.

"Earrings. I bought Quinn some earrings. And a dress." Heather said. "I want to see them on her."

"Cool. What did you bring me?" he teased.

"Zippo," Zander quipped.

"He's a liar. We brought you a towel." She left the kitchen and came back to toss a towel identical to Quinn's in his face. "Enjoy."

He impressed Quinn by looking the towel over, wrapping it around himself and saying seriously, "I love it. Thank you."

Quinn exchanged the earrings she wore for the new ones. "How do they look?" she asked.

"They're perfect," Heather gushed. "I love the way they hang against your neck."

Quinn swished her head back and forth. The earrings brushed against her skin. She wanted to go look at them, but her knees were still weak from the shock of Tyson's arrival.

"Let's see the dress," Heather urged.

"Ya, let's," Tyson added.

"I'm sure it fits fine." She picked up her soda and took a sip. "I'll try it on later."

"Please," Heather begged.

Reluctantly, she went into the master bedroom and changed. She stared at herself in the mirror. The bright color highlighted her eyes and seemed to make her skin glow. She had to admit that she looked lovely.

"What do you think?" she asked when she returned to the kitchen.

"Wow," Zander exclaimed. "You look great. I wish I'd seen you in that before I hooked up with her," he teased and jabbed a thumb at Heather.

"Jerk," Heather responded with no hint of anger. "It looks amazing on you. It's the perfect color."

"You look very nice," Tyson said solemnly. "Very nice."

She ignored his praise. She'd said she was shunning him. She wasn't giving him one word that wasn't needed from her. He was lucky she'd slipped up and greeted him. "I love the way it fits, and the fabric is so soft. It's a bit cool for today. I think I'll get back into my sweater."

Heather followed her down the hall and into the bedroom, the way best friends do. She closed the door behind them. "What's up with you?" she demanded. "You're being rude to Ty. I thought you liked him. You were spending a lot of time with him before we left."

"Wedding business only."

"What's up, Quinn? I thought you liked him. That's why I invited you at the same time." She seemed genuinely puzzled.

"I do. I did. Don't bother trying to put us together. He's made it perfectly clear that I'm not good enough for him." She blinked away tears as she pulled off the dress. She pivoted slightly to hide her minuscule baby bump.

"You've gained weight."

"I guess now that I'm not running with Tyson during his appointments three times a week, I'm plumping up again." She dipped her head to hide the color in her cheeks.

"Oh." Heather stared at her. "Oh my gosh. Are you pregnant?" she whispered the final word.

No sense denying it. Half the town knew already. Okay, maybe not that many. But this was her best friend. "Yes."

"Does Duke know?"

"No, and I'm not telling him either."

"I'm good with that. Who else knows?"

"Can we just drop it? I don't want to talk about it."

Heather gave her a long studying look, her eyes compassionate. "Are you happy about it at least?"

"I am. I wasn't prepared for this. I have no idea how I'll manage as a single mom, but I already love Little Bean."

"Congratulations!" She rushed over and threw her arms around Quinn. "I'm happy for you. Who knows, maybe I'll get pregnant soon and we can raise our babies together."

Quinn laughed at her enthusiasm. "Are you planning to?"

"Not really, no. In the future for sure, but no immediate plans. I'm so thrilled for you. You'll be an amazing mom. You're so kind and compassionate, and you've got a huge heart." She stepped back. "Sorry about you and Tyson. I had hoped …"

"Me too. But that's all water under the bridge and the bridge is burned down and the water dammed up. Life goes on." She stood face to face with her friend, looking her right in the eye. "Seriously. I'm fine."

"You're not fine. But you will be." They hugged again. "Get changed. I'm starving."

Quinn didn't think she could eat, her stomach was roiling. Again. But she put on a brave face as they returned to the kitchen.

"I got everything ready in the dining room," Zander said and kissed Heather on the cheek. "We can eat anytime." He gave Quinn a long, steady look, shook his head, and led them into the dining room. Ty followed behind.

The long table was set with two place settings on each side. Zander pulled out a chair for Heather. Tyson, in turn, pulled out Quinn's. She sat without comment, and he sat beside her.

The polished oak table was beautiful with carved edges. A white cloth ran down the center. There were unlit candles on each end of the serving dishes. She prayed that nobody would light them and turn the casual meal into a romantic one.

She sucked in a steadying breath and instantly regretted it. Tyson's familiar and unique scent washed over her waking her senses

and stirring her body. Dang it. She thought she was safe beside
him because that way she wasn't going to be looking at him. His
knee brushed hers. It was impossible to tell who moved away more
quickly.

This was going to be a long meal. The food was probably delicious. She had no idea. Everything tasted the same. At least what she
managed to choke down. Thankfully, the servings of chicken were
small, and everything else was served family style. She served herself
tiny portions, pretended to eat, and shifted things around on her
plate.

Most of the conversation revolved around the wedding and honeymoon so she didn't have to put in much discussion. It was a good
thing too. Her mind was so caught up in Tyson. Thinking about
him. Avoiding his accidental touches. Listening to the sound of his
voice.

It was torture.

It was bliss.

She jumped up. "I'm sorry. I gotta go. I just remembered I have
a ..." she floundered for a second. "A Zoom meeting." She picked
up her plate. "Thanks for the gifts. Dinner was amazing, as always.
Heather, you're my favorite chef of all time." She put her plate on
the kitchen counter, grabbed her purse and gifts, and bolted for the
door.

Chapter Eighteen

D inner last night had been horrid. Not the food, which was delicious, as always. The honeymoon stories were interesting as well. But sitting beside Quinn, smelling her fresh, summer scent, feeling the heat of her body beside his. Touching her with his knee. Her hair had been scooped back in a floaty ponytail revealing her long neck and the sweet curve where it met her shoulders. A tiny strand of hair had come loose near her ear. It was all he could do not to tuck it away for her.

The earrings Heather gave her dangled enticingly along her neck, inviting him closer. Begging him to place his lips against her warm skin. Pure delicious torture.

It was bad, but not as bad as her complete and total insistence that he didn't exist. She had said exactly one word to him. His name.

After that first reluctant greeting, it was like he didn't exist. It hurt. She didn't even ask him to pass the salt. Nothing. Not another word. When she left, he'd stared straight ahead. He refused to watch her leave.

He did not miss her.

He wasn't tempted to call her. At least not more than twenty times a day. He was not waking in the middle of the night, wanting to chat to her about his day.

Fiddlesticks.

At least today was Saturday. He'd done his physio. Not without thinking about her. He'd cleaned the kitchen and thought about the tea she loved so much. His social media feed was filled with images of his friend's kids, making him think about the child she carried.

Even when she wasn't around, there was no escaping her.

Early afternoon arrived and he was depressed and unaccountably angry. He headed for the grocery store. He'd do some shopping and then go visit his mother. Maybe take her out for supper.

As always happened on Saturday, the grocery store was jammed. He took the last cart and slowly trudged up and down the aisles, weaving around carts and chatting patrons as he picked up the items on his mental shopping list. At work he kept physical lists, on paper, on his computer. Groceries, he played fast and loose, buying whatever inspired him in the moment. He didn't bake, so he didn't need to stock those supplies.

He greeted a few parents as he walked along and was avoided by two of his tougher students. He could live with that. Nobody said they had to like him, as long as they abided by school rules. On the third aisle, as he was choosing between two sugary cereals, his only real vice, a familiar but unwelcome voice called, "Mr. Bellamie."

Steeling himself, he turned toward Mrs. Gilbert. She looked the same as always, starched blouse, dressy pants creased by an iron to a razor-sharp edge, and a dour expression on her face. "Mrs. Gilbert. Lovely to see you. You look nice today."

She preened for a second before casting a disdainful glare at the boxes in his hands. "I hope you don't eat that."

"Indeed, I do. It's my one food vice. A small bowl as a treat twice a week." He resisted the urge to tell her to mind her own business. As a board member, she deserved respect, even if she wasn't a pleasant human being.

"Are you interested in a job as coach of the football team? I'm told you have the experience."

Why would he leave his position as principal for a lesser job? He'd have to be nuts. "No, I don't believe I am. I'm quite content where I am."

She sniffed and her face puckered as if she smelled something terrible. "Well," she stepped closer and dropped her voice. "I've heard that girl you've been tom catting around with is pregnant. What are you going to do about it? Since there's been no wedding announcement, I assume you don't care and don't plan to marry her. For the school principal and a man with his application in for a board position, it seems highly irresponsible. The board needs people who stand up for their beliefs. Strong family-oriented people. Think about that."

Lord, save him from meddling old women. While he wanted to tell her off, he knew better.

"Quinn Davidson is a respectable young woman. We spent time together while working on my brother's wedding. Zander married Quinn's best friend. We were not, and are not, dating. I have no idea if she is pregnant or not. But, if she is, the child is not mine." He nodded to punctuate his statement. "Good day, Mrs. Gilbert. I hope you enjoy the rest of your weekend. He tossed both boxes of cereal in his cart as an act of defiance and pushed gently past her.

She had her nerve. Implying that he'd abandon a pregnant woman. And implying he was unfit to be on the board but fit to be a football coach. The logic in her conversation was definitely lacking. He'd probably killed his chances of getting the board position by being snippy. But who could blame him? She was sour and mean and needed to retire.

He stopped and closed his eyes for a second. He had to calm down or he'd ram his cart into something.

A soft touch landed on his arm. His eyes flew open, and he jumped back.

"Tyson, are you okay?" Quinn stared up at him with concerned eyes. Oh, she was a sight for sore eyes. His anger faded as he stared at her.

"I'm fine. I just had a run-in with a busybody. Thank you." He wanted to go back three seconds and not pull away from her touch. "I'm fine. Thanks for asking. Have a nice day." He walked away. As he turned the corner toward the next aisle, he peeked back at her. She stared at him with a puzzled look.

He didn't care.

He did not care.

His mind whispered the words over and over in a vain attempt to convince himself. It didn't work. He did care. He missed her.

Once he was home and had his groceries put away, he called and offered to bring his mother dinner from her favorite restaurant. When she suggested going out, he declined claiming he just wanted some uninterrupted time with her. Despite her earlier meddling in his non-relationship with Quinn, she'd be a sympathetic listener and good company.

"How was your week?" she asked as soon as they sat at the table.

"Busy as always, but good." He sliced into his halibut as she tasted her salmon. "I've applied for the board position. Mr. Kavanaugh is retiring next year. They've already listed his position."

"You'll get it for sure." She patted his hand. "You're perfect for it."

"I don't know, Mom." He related his encounter with Mrs. Gilbert. "Then, in the parking lot, I ran into Mrs. Jepson. That woman is the worst gossip. She flat out informed me that Quinn was pregnant and that I better do the right thing." He dropped his fork, and it clattered off his plate onto the floor. He picked it up and carefully set it down again. "Why can't people mind their own business?"

"I ask myself that every day." Her tone was ironic. "But I have to say, you've been miserable for weeks now. Ever since you stopped seeing Quinn. Maybe you should 'do the right thing'." She made air quotes around the last phrase.

Great. Now his mother was piling on. He'd hoped she'd do better tonight.

"You'd probably be happier. You like her. You miss her. You're more than compatible."

"Anyway. I had dinner with Heather and Zander last night. Sounds like their trip was fun. Have you seen them yet?"

"Nice change of subject. Subtle, son. Subtle. Point taken. I'll drop it for now." She picked up her fork and ate a few bites.

Glad the conversation was done, he picked up his own, though he was no longer hungry.

"But" she added, "consider whether you'd be happier with the job, or the woman. It's okay if life plans change." She resumed eating, leaving him to think about her words.

And he did.

For seven long days and nights.

Every morning, he woke up wondering how Quinn was feeling. Was she managing okay? Was she eating the right things and getting enough rest? Did she need anything? Was she as grumpy as he was?

There had to be something he could do to get her out of his mind, and for good. He pulled out his phone and scrolled his dating apps. Over one hundred women had marked him as a prospective date. Exactly zero of them interested him. He scrolled through dozens of listings on three different apps for over half an hour before he gave up.

He pushed away from his desk and stared around his office. It was an enormous room in his walkout basement. Outside was dark except for the solar lights in his yard. One lonely light illuminated his pool. He switched off the interior lights and moved to one of the wing chairs nestled into the bookshelf-lined corner. It was the perfect reading nook. All it needed was someone to keep him company. He stared out the window. He couldn't go on like this. He needed to make a change to get his life back in order before it totally spiraled out of control.

Head back, eyes closed, he tried to banish Quinn from his mind. Finally, he drifted into an uneasy, dream filled sleep.

He woke with a start and an aching neck. It was still dark outside. A glance at his watch told him it was four in the morning. Too early to get up. But he was too uneasy to return to sleep. He wandered into the kitchen and poured himself an enormous bowl of sugary cereal. Wouldn't Quinn laugh at him eating pure sugar? He shoveled the cereal in, not wanting it, but needing to do something as he pondered what came next in his life.

All the advice he'd been given over the past weeks rolled around in his head. Marry Quinn. Walk away. Become a coach instead of an administrator. Leave town. Stay. Stop serial dating in the city. Settle down.

Abruptly, in a flash of insight he knew exactly what he wanted to do. The brief glimmer he'd felt growing in his mind weeks ago burst forth as a plan. He abandoned his bowl on the table, something he never did, and headed for the shower.

Chapter Nineteen

"Y ou're leaving?"

"Sorry, I'll put in my two weeks' notice. But I'm leaving Half Moon Bay. It's something I feel I need to do," Quinn slid her resignation letter across the desk toward the hospital administrator.

"You've had no complaints. You're an asset to the hospital. Is there anything we can do to convince you to stay?"

"I'm afraid not. I've made my decision. It's time to go." Beyond time. She couldn't live another day knowing she might run into Tyson every time she stepped out of her apartment.

"What prompted this move?"

"It's personal." She did not want to get into this, but she couldn't be rude and risk a bad reference letter.

"Ah, the baby." The administrator, Stella Ardois, shook her head sadly. She was in her late forties and had a husband and four kids. "We don't care that you aren't in a relationship, or that you'll be a single mother. We have several single mothers and single fathers on staff. It isn't the stigma it was decades ago. Your marital status is irrelevant. You do understand that, right?"

"I appreciate that, but it doesn't change my decision." Being a single mom was a worry, but not because of public opinion. It just figured that the news, though unannounced, had gotten back to her boss already.

"Can you stay until you're due to start your new position? It would be enormously helpful."

She wanted to leave today. But in truth, she didn't have a new position. She was looking, but so far nothing had come up that would suit her needs. She was heading into motherhood without a job prospect on the horizon. She would be wise to work here until she found one. She'd only put in her notice to force herself to start the process of moving on from Tyson.

She sighed. "Okay. I'll work until my start date."

"And when is that?" Stella typed something into her computer.

"Honestly? I don't know. I don't have another position yet. But I am looking." She stared at the carpet and the dust on her sensible work shoes.

"What? You aren't serious, are you?"

Quinn looked up. "I am. Things are—complicated. I need to leave Half Moon Bay. As soon as possible. For my own sanity."

"So, it isn't just the baby." She paused thoughtfully. "Can I tell you something, in confidence? It's probably not a secret anymore, but I don't want it blabbed around. If you know what I mean."

"No secrets in a small town." She shrugged. "But yes, I'll keep your confidence." Stella was always all business, but at the same time, she loved to tell stories.

"When I came to Half Moon Bay, I was a single mother of one adorable six-year-old boy. I started as assistant administrator."

Quinn nodded. Nothing new there.

"I didn't move for work. I moved to get away from a situation like yours. I was in love with a man. A married man. I had to get away."

Quinn was shocked. *This upright administrator had dated a married man.* She kept quiet, though she didn't understand how someone could do that. She was hardly one to judge, having pined for Tyson the entire time she'd been hooking up with Duke.

"We worked together. He was a doctor. We didn't date. But, through work committees, we spent a lot of time together. I grew to care for him. Too much. He never gave a single inkling or hint that he was interested in me. Not one."

"What did you do?" Quinn asked, seeing similarities with her own life. Her heart went out to the younger version of Stella who had been forced to flee or compromise her morals.

"I left. Though I waited until I found this job before I put in my notice. I came here with my son. Best decision I ever made."

"And the guy?"

Stella's face lit up and she laughed. "I married him."

"What? How?"

"He came after me. Not until he was divorced. First by email. Then, in person. Seems he was waiting for that divorce to go through before he approached me. Their marriage was withering before we met, and he had the decency and respect for his ex to wait until they were completely divorced to approach me."

Quinn wanted to swoon for the romance of it all. "That's incredible."

"It really is. We're very happy. We have four children now. The oldest is fourteen, the youngest is six. But you probably know all that."

"I did. But I had no idea of your history. Just that you were married to a family practice doctor."

"Well, I couldn't hire him. Nepotism would get me fired by the board. But we made it work and we're happy."

"Congratulations. Though I don't know why you told me this." She expected Stella to have a reason, nobody shared something that personal without one.

"Why? Because I value you as an employee. Our patients consistently request you. Keeping you on is good business. But I want you to know that sometimes there is hope. I've seen you with the Bellamie boy. Tyson, isn't it? There is a spark there. I don't want you to let that get away. Give it time. He cares for you. I saw it when you were together. He couldn't keep his eyes off you at the wedding. Perhaps he'll figure it out."

"I know he cares. He's shown it a hundred ways. But I can't take it any longer. He has issues, blinders, that he's unwilling to remove." She shrugged as if it didn't matter. "He's putting his career first. Just like he did with football. He gives his everything to the things he does, no matter how small. Right now, that's his career. I can't wait until he has the time or inclination to be with me. So, I'm taking this child away where I won't face constant reminders of him. This isn't Tyson's baby," she added for clarification.

She sighed. There was no way she'd outrun the memories, or the pain in her heart, but she had to try.

"I respect your need to protect yourself," Stella said, "but please think it over, and know that you have a job here. Always." She stood, a sure sign the meeting was over. "Thanks for giving me advance notice but do consider staying on instead of leaving town. Half Moon Bay needs more people like you."

"I'll think about it," Quinn lied. She had no intention of hanging around waiting for her heart to be sliced to ribbons with each sighting of Tyson. *Fiddlesticks! Her heart couldn't stand this.* "Thanks for seeing me."

"Oh, one last thing." Stella paused. "Today I received a letter from Mr. Bellamie saying that he was extremely impressed with your skill and professionalism. There was a full paragraph, a rather long one, praising your talents. He credits you completely for his rehab. He included a sizable donation to your department. It's earmarked for helping low-income families afford rehab."

"Oh?" *Why had he done that?* "Thanks for letting me know." She returned to her department and studied the file for her last patient of the day. It was a tough case. A fourteen-year-old girl had lost her leg in a car accident. She had a prosthesis but hated its utilitarian look. Summer was coming and Quinn wanted her patient to feel comfortable in summer wear.

"Rose-Marie, come on back." Sullen and unwilling to make eye contact, the petite brunette followed her. "How are you today?"

"Life sucks."

Quinn barely refrained from rolling her eyes. "We're doing something different today. I think you might like this."

"Whatevs. You're the boss." The response was curt to the point of rudeness, but Quinn recognized the glimmer of hope and interest.

Quinn picked up a chunk of carboard and a bag she had prepped earlier. She set them in a wheelchair and led Rose-Marie outside through a staff entrance.

"I don't want to do my stuff out here. Someone might see."

"Crap happens. But we won't be working out today. I have something else planned." She spread a ratty blanket on the dull brown grass outside the door. Take a seat. Do you want help to get down?" The process of getting up and down off the floor or the ground was still awkward for Rose-Marie, but she would not offend her by giving unwanted assistance.

"I've got it," the teen snapped. "I'm not helpless."

"No, you are actually very capable." She smiled encouragingly. "Can you slip out of your prosthesis for me?"

"What? Why?"

"Play along, for me. Will ya?"

Rose-Marie dug under her long workout shorts, unhooked the limb, and set it on the blanket. Shorts were a requirement for her physio as Quinn had to keep a constant watch on the amputation site for irritation or swelling. They draped a soft towel over her leg to hide the stump to prevent Rose-Marie from being embarrassed if anyone came along.

"What are we doing? I can't do anything without my leg."

Quinn settled down beside her. "That's not true," she said softly. "You can do a lot without it. Your life has changed so much, it must be very difficult for you. But today we're doing something fun."

"Ya, what's that?" she snarked.

"You hate your prosthesis because it is ugly, right?"

"You know that." She crossed her arms over her chest.

"I also know that your parents can't afford a custom colored one. So ..." she trailed off and dug into her bag and extracted two cans of spray paint with a flourish. "We're going to paint it."

"Mom would kill me!"

"No, she won't. I asked if we could do this. I did some research, and this paint will be tacky in twenty minutes and dry in half an hour, and it's safe for the materials of your leg. Want to have a go? I've got red, blue, gold, silver, pink, purple, and teal. Pick your color." She spilled the rest of the spray cans on the blanket.

"Really?" She stared at all the cans. "This must have cost a fortune. Paint is expensive."

"Actually, the paint was donated. You aren't the only patient I have that needs an upgrade." She smiled. "What do you say, should we jazz this thing up?"

"Yes!"

"We probably won't finish today, but we can get a couple coats on for sure. Where shall we start?"

Laughing together, they painted the prosthesis with swirls of color and a few random dots of gold and silver. It was wild and crazy, but Rose-Marie was ecstatic by the time they finished. By spraying some paint into a plastic dish, they were able to use a paintbrush for small details.

Quinn was going to investigate if Tyson's donation could be used to fund a better leg for Rose-Marie.

Ninety minutes later, their time was more than up.

"The paint might still be tacky in places," she warned. "We'll get you to the car in the wheelchair. Your mom is bringing some plastic to set it on until it dries. I'd stand it up when you get home, so the tacky bits don't rub off on something. And wait until tomorrow to put it on."

"Okay."

"Would you like help into the chair?"

"Please."

She took Rose-Marie and her prosthesis directly to the front entry where her mother waited to pick her up. This moment was, by far, the happiest she'd ever seen the teen, and the moment warmed her heart.

"Hey, there."

Quinn turned toward the familiar voice.

"Mr. Bellamie," Rose-Marie exclaimed. "Check out my leg." She held her prosthesis out for him to see.

Her mother looked as shocked as Quinn felt.

"Great paint job? Did you do that?"

"I did. Quinn helped. It was her idea."

Tyson smiled at them both. "Great work ladies. Rose-Marie, maybe you should consider a career in art. You've got talent."

"She does," her mother enthused. "She paints and draws at home, though she won't show anyone except family. She's actually very good."

"I would be honored if you ever wanted to gift me with the chance to see your work," Tyson said, seriously. "If you are as good as your mother says, I have contacts in several great art schools. And maybe there are some classes at school you might be interested in."

Rose-Marie blushed bright red. "Really? Maybe you could see some stuff."

"Let me know if you want me to look, and when. I'm happy to help you out. Great job on the leg." His smile was a thousand watts and burned right into Quinn's heart.

"Quinn, I was wondering if I could talk to you. I'm having a bit of trouble with my knee."

"Sure, meet me in the physio department. I can spare a few minutes, though technically, I'm off the clock."

He turned to Rose-Marie and her mother. "Let me know about a private viewing, ladies. I'd be honored to see your creations. See you at school, Rose-Marie."

He walked away, headed for Quinn's office.

"Rose-Marie, you've been holding out on me," Quinn teased. "No wonder your leg looks so amazing." It truly was a work of art. "You're an artist. Good for you! I'll see you on Tuesday after school. If we get through your workout quickly enough, we can touch up the leg if it needs it."

"Can I borrow that paint?" she asked. "I could finish at home. I'll bring the leftovers back."

"Absolutely. Now, let's get you into the car."

She procrastinated meeting Tyson by watching them until they drove around the corner out of sight. She didn't want to meet with him. She wasn't sure her heart could take it. Straightening her spine, she turned and inched her way toward her office.

Chapter Twenty

T yson stared around the deserted physio department. It was nearly six. Most of the staff and patients were long gone. He hadn't meant to stop here. He'd been heading toward the inn for dinner with his family. He'd taken a detour down a side street and back alley to avoid some road construction. When he saw Quinn's Kia in the lot, he pulled in. He was at the front doors before he realized what he was doing and where he was going.

He'd panicked and said his knee hurt.

Liar, liar, pants on fire.

Now, he'd have to submit to an exam. If she showed up at all. Who was he kidding? Quinn was the epitome of professional. She'd come, and she'd be polite even though she probably and rightly felt that he was a jack-hole.

He paced back and forth in the waiting area, nerves ate at his stomach, making it ache. He should just go.

"Doesn't look like your knee hurts that badly," she said from the doorway, her tone completely professional. "I don't see any signs of a limp."

"It's ... it's intermittent pain."

She raised one eyebrow. "You should make an appointment for an assessment. Or you could see your doctor for a referral."

She was right, he was bucking the system, and doing so without thought. "I could. I should," he agreed.

She looked at him with questions and doubts in her mind. There was no doubt she didn't want to assess his fake problem, though professionalism probably kept her from saying anything rude.

"Fine. I'll assess your leg and book you with one of my colleagues for physio." She strode down the hall, waving for him to follow. She stopped outside an exam room. "In you go. There's a gown on the shelf or a pair of shorts in the next pile. Get changed and I'll be back in a minute."

All her kindness and sympathy were gone. She was a stone-cold pro with zero empathy. He never would have guessed she was capable of such a frigid manner. The more he thought about it, the more he realized it was a façade. One he'd never breach.

She knocked on the door. "Come in. I'm ready."

She entered and without sparing him a glance slipped her access card into the computer and logged onto his file. She entered something. She pivoted on her swivel stool. "What's the problem?"

"Um. Er. It hurts." Oh, man. Could you be more lame?

"When you walk? When you sit? When you jog? I'll need specifics, Mr. Bellamie." She reached out and patted the exam table he hovered beside. "Hop up here."

He lifted himself onto the table and sat, legs dangling.

"I'm going to palpate both knees and check for swelling, Mr. Bellamie." She rolled forward and placed her hands on his injured knee.

Electricity jolted through him. He jumped back and gasped.

"Did that hurt?" She asked, no sympathy in her voice.

"No. You startled me."

She stared up at him, a yeah, right look on her face. "Why are you here?"

"I need physio." He groaned silently, totally chickening out.

"Bull cookies. Why are you here?"

"My knee hurts. I'm worried I might have hurt it."

"Where does it hurt?" she asked, clearly not believing him.

"Here." He touched one of his tiny surgery scars. "And I think it's swollen back here."

She palpated his knee, and he managed not to jerk away from the sweet warmth of her touch. She checked both knees.

"I'm not feeling any inflammation. Mr. Bellamie, can you hop down and walk to the door and back? Let me check your gait."

He slid off the table and walked to the door, half tempted to fake a limp rather than admit he was there on false pretenses. He was such a coward.

"You have no limp. You have no swelling." She paused and looked up at his face as he turned back around. "What you do have is nothing. Nothing but crap. There's no need to show up at my work to harass me. Get. Out. She stabbed her index finger at the door. Out now, before I call hospital security."

She stood and stepped toward the door. He stepped in front of her.

"Really?" She plopped her hands on her sweet curving hips. "Now it's getting physical. I thought better of you, Tyson."

"Ah. Finally, my first name."

"Get out of my way."

He held up his hands in surrender. "Give me five minutes. Please."

She closed her eyes and sighed. The sigh cut like a knife to the heart. "Get dressed, meet me in my office when you are decent." The way she snarled the last word left no doubt that she thought him incapable of being decent. Her face was a mask of hurt and distress.

She eased the door shut behind her. Somehow the gentle gesture hurt more than if she'd slammed it in his face. As quickly as he could, he jumped back into his jeans, straightened himself up and went to her office. He stood beside the door, just out of sight to steel his nerves.

She was talking. Probably on the phone since he heard no response in the pauses between her words. Rudely, and without remorse, or at least not much, he eavesdropped.

"Tyson is in my office," she hissed, her voice barely audible. There was a short silence. "I kicked him out of my life, and he shows up faking an injury. He's got gall." More silence. "Why the heck would I give him a chance? Heather, you're insane. He's not a good guy. He's a jerk. An epic, lower than a slug's belly, dirty rotten stinking jerk. I hope his boy bits fall off."

He winced, covered himself and waited for whatever shot was coming next.

"I don't know what he wants, but I'm not buying whatever crap he's selling. I waited four years for him to notice me. Finally, he does, but I'm not good enough. Well, he can get stuffed."

Silence reigned for a full thirty seconds.

"Fine. I'll call you later. Bye." The phone clanged on the cradle.

He waited for a count of twelve and he started whistling softly. Slowly, he raised the volume so it would sound like he was coming closer. He knocked on the partially open door.

"Ya. Come in."

He stood in front of her tidy desk feeling like he was an errant knight outside a castle wall, and longing for the maiden inside. He looked around, noting the certificates on the wall, the plants in the window, the bulletin board filled with hand-drawn pictures and thank you notes. He cleared his throat. "Quinn ..."

She said nothing, just looked up at him, eyes wary, hands hidden under the desk. She shifted slightly. At length, she nodded for him to continue.

"Quinn. There's nothing wrong with my knee."

She looked at him as if to say, do you think I'm stupid?

It was awkward, standing high above her. So, he perched on the edge of a chair and scooted it forward. He placed his forearms on her desk. "I stopped in on impulse. I had meant to come see you, just not in a public place, and certainly not at work. I apologize for making it awkward." His mouth was cottony, and he'd have given his truck for a glass of water. He had hoped she'd say something but she remained mute, and as still as a statue. He had no choice but to carry on. Words, excuses, and apologies tumbled about in his head, each pushing for dominance.

"I think we should get married." He nearly groaned at the abrupt declaration. Her laughter was like a slap in the face.

"I think you should go." She pushed back her chair but didn't stand. "You've humiliated me enough to last a lifetime. Her eyes glimmered.

Tears.

"That came out wrong. I like you, Quinn. Hear me out." He rubbed his thumbs against his index fingers. I like you a lot. Getting married would make your life easier. You could stop worrying about your future, and your baby's future."

"And what, exactly, do you get out of this magnanimous offer?" Her clenched fists rose to the top of the desk. She placed them down gently, though they remained white-knuckled.

"I get a wife."

"Thank you for your selfless offer. I'll pass. Have a nice day."

"Quinn, don't be hasty."

"Oh, hasty like you deciding I'm unfit to be around? Like I'm not worth dating? Like I'd ruin your life?" She stood, shoulders tense, hands fisted, eyes flashing with angry fire. "And then coming back as if suddenly I'm okay? What's the matter Tyson, did your prospective board members tell you to get married? Are you just trying to ramp up your reputation?" She glared. "Leave. Now. Don't come back ever."

Frozen by her unexpected rejection, he stared back.

"Leave. Before I call security. I'm done with you. Do. Not. Come. Back." She reached for the phone.

"Think about it. Please." He backed out of her office and walked away, heart thumping, knees trembling, heart aching.

How had that gone so badly?

Fresh off his honeymoon or not, Zander was the only man who could help.

Chapter Twenty-One

Quinn made three stops on her way home. The grocery store for ice cream and cake. The pizza joint for a carb-loading feast of pizza and garlic toast. The liquor store for dealcoholized wine. She might not be able to get drunk, but dang it, she could pretend.

An hour later, totally bloated, disappointed in the lack of buzz from the wine, she flipped through the television, looking for a tragic movie to watch. Some random tearjerker. She had yet to cry after this last, massive insult. Though tears threatened, over and over, none had spilled. She needed a good cry. A pity fest for a while, and then she'd pull up her big girl panties and move on. Why wouldn't the tears come?

Someone knocked on her apartment door. Her elderly next-door neighbor often popped over unannounced for tea. Perfect, she

needed the distraction. She trudged to the door, her slippers dragging with every step. She flipped the deadbolt and opened the door.

"Oh, honey, are you okay?" Heather strode closer and embraced
Quinn in a warm, comforting hug.

"No. What are you doing here?" She leaned into her friend's arms
for a moment. "Come in." She tromped back to her spot on the
couch, nearly tripping on the plush area rug that had shifted at some
point.

"I brought the cavalry," she said, shedding her light jacket. "Come
in, gals."

"What? Who?" Quinn asked. Heather's new sisters-in-law came
in. Lexi and Sammi were a surprise. "What are you all doing here?"
Quinn knew them but hadn't ever considered them friends.

"Girl," Heather said, "You're practically family now. That makes
your problems our problems. "We're here to support you. Nobody
should go through a bad breakup alone."

Quinn stared at them, unable to believe they'd step up for a virtual
stranger just because she was interested in one of their relatives.
She knew them from the wedding, but not well. "Please tell me
you didn't invite Beth." Having Tyson's mother show up would be
humiliating.

"We did not. This is a sisters' thing. Now, we brought snacks."
She pulled a cheesecake from her tote. Sammi set a plate of veggies
and a bowl of dip on the table.

"Where's the kitchen?" Lexi asked. "I've got soda and juice for
fake mimosas. In deference to your condition, we'll forgo the alcohol
and save it for after the baby comes."

Quinn burst into tears. Two warm bodies settled beside her on
the sofa and put their arms across her shoulders. A box of tissues

appeared on her lap. "Thanks." She sobbed. "I appreciate it, but I'm not family. And I won't ever be."

"Nonsense." She patted Quinn's back. "Tyson's at our place right now, complaining to Zander. Honey, he adores you. He's an idiot and has no idea what he wants or how to talk to you, but he does care."

"Ya, he cares about his reputation." She refused to give in to the glimmer of hope shimmering in her heart. "I quit my job today," she confessed. "I'm leaving Half Moon Bay as soon as I find a new job."

"What?" Heather and Sammi exclaimed in unison.

"Oh, don't do that," Lexi said coming into the room with a pitcher of juice, and four glasses on an unfamiliar tray. She must have brought the tray with her. She set the tray on the coffee table and smoothed back her dark hair.

Sammi added, "Never let a man run you off. I nearly made that mistake myself. Stick to your life. No man is worth destroying your life for."

"Moving will *fix* my life," Quinn disagreed.

"Don't leave. He'll come around," Heather said. "He just needs to figure out his head. Men aren't good at dealing with emotions."

"He proposed today. He just showed up at work, faking an injury and proposed." Quinn sobbed.

"That's good, isn't it?" Lexi asked.

"He said, and I quote, "Getting married would make your life easier." Can you imagine the nerve. What was he thinking? I don't want to be married to make my life easier. I want to marry because I'm in love and because he loves me." She pounded her fist on her thigh. "Oh, I'm so mad. He said it like he was making this huge sacrifice and doing me an enormous favor." She burst into a fresh wave of gasping tears. An emotional band wrapped around her chest growing tighter and tighter with every breath.

"Wouldn't it be okay to marry him? You do love him. I know he loves you. If not, he'd grow to love you. I'm sure of it." Heather patted her shoulder.

The kindly meant gesture did nothing but irritate Quinn even further. She jumped up and paced, nearly tripping on her floppy slippers. She kicked them off. One ricocheted off her television. "Am I wrong to want him to love me?" She didn't wait for an answer. "A couple weeks ago he said he couldn't date me because he had a reputation to maintain. How is that different now? If we married, his precious reputation would still be in a mess, at least by his standards. He'd still have married a woman who dated too many men. Is pregnant to boot. Maybe he wants a virgin, or an angel dropped straight from heaven."

She stomped her foot. "Everyone in town thinks it's his baby. That's the only reason he proposed. Lesser of two evils. I won't, I can't, marry to save his reputation."

Her companions were silent. Sammi finally spoke up. "I think you're right. He'd come to regret being forced into a relationship with you. I know it. I think the solution is to give him time to realize that he can't live without you."

"Why are men so stupid?" Lexi asked. "They can never see what's right in front of them, especially if it is a good woman." All four women laughed a bit sourly.

Somehow, the wry comment made Quinn feel better. She wasn't healed, not by a long shot, but she was lifted out of her pity party. She might even consider their advice. She didn't have a job yet, so Tyson had a bit of time to wake up and realize what a treasure she was. But if the words I love you didn't appear in his proposal, all bets were off.

"You know what you should do? Take an ad out and publicly declare that he's not the father," Heather joked.

"That would just humiliate her further," Sammi disagreed.

Heather raised her hands in surrender. "I was joking. But you can bet your bacon that I'll be making that fact clear to any gossip who approaches me. Not that it's any of their business."

"I appreciate that." Quinn sighed. "I already had to tell my boss the baby wasn't Tyson's. I do wish it was." She clamped her hand over her mouth. She had not meant to say that.

"He will be a good father when he comes around," Lexi said. "He's so good with Ella and his students and their parents adore him. He's firm but caring. He does go the extra mile for them."

"He was so great with Rose-Marie yesterday at the hospital."

"Her accident was so tragic," Heather said. Everyone in town was familiar with Rose-Marie and the car that had careened into the convenience store on her third day of work.

"We painted her prosthesis as part of her rehab. We were walking out when Ty showed up. He offered to look at her art and maybe help her apply to art schools," Quinn said. "She opened up to him a little bit. She's been so closed off for so long. I've been working with her for eight months now and she's only just starting to talk freely with me. He'll be a great dad and husband for some family."

"He'll be yours," Heather insisted. "I've seen him moping and whining to Zander more than once." She chuckled. "It was pretty cool, in a weird way."

"He better come around soon," Quinn decreed. She picked up a glass. "Here's to idiot men, may they finally come to their senses." And sooner, rather than later, she silently added.

Chapter Twenty-Two

"I can't understand why she didn't accept my proposal," Tyson grumbled. He sounded like a broken record and didn't care. He thought he had it all figured out and then she went and refused his proposal. He leaned against the veterinary clinic wall, watching Zander do his final check on his overnight patients. His vet assistant would work the night shift and call him if there were any issues.

"Are you nearly done?" Ty asked. "I need a beer."

"Since your grumbling chased off my new wife, you can feed me. Order something to eat. Food first, beer later." He slipped the rabbit he was holding back into its pen and latched the door. "I can't stand listening to you whine like a girl, at least not on an empty stomach."

"Dude. I listened to your woes about Heather." He punched in an order for pizza. The pizza place was the only restaurant in town that would deliver this far out. Five miles was nothing in the city, but here it was too far for most food places.

"Come on, Ty. You know what you have to do. You know what you want."

"I want to be administrator of the school board. On the board to start with, and head of the board in a few years. Eventually, I'd like to head the state school board." He refused to voice anything about Quinn.

"And your personal life?" Zander scrubbed his hands and eased a groggy Persian cat from its cage.

"I proposed. She declined. I'll go back to dating."

"You're an idiot." He checked the cat's heartbeat without lifting his head. "Quinn is a lovely woman. We dated a couple of times. She's not my type. No sparks. But she is smart, kind, and compassionate. She's got a great sense of humor. She's employed. People like her. I don't see what your issue is ... unless it's the chip on your shoulder or your big block of a head."

"Yeah, she's perfect. She's hot too." He sighed. This conversation was not going the way he wanted it to. "But she ..."

"She what?" His brother spared him a quick glance as he charted his findings on the animals.

"She had that on again, off again thing with Duke. Duke!" He couldn't keep his revulsion for the man from his tone. "And she's dated dozens of men."

"And?"

"And I have a reputation to maintain if I want that job."

"You're an idiot. Half the town knows that you go out of town to date every weekend. Just because you aren't doing it here, it doesn't mean nobody knows. It's probably worse because it looks like you're trying to hide it." Zander washed his hands again. "Honestly, I don't know why you're so concerned. Either you get the board job, or you don't. Happiness doesn't come from work. Not one single person on their deathbed has ever said they didn't work enough."

Ty scraped his hands over his face and scratched his beard. "Moving up in my career is important to me."

"You never struck me as the administrator type. I'm surprised you gave up being the Phys Ed teacher and coaching to sit at a desk all day. Truthfully, I can't believe you didn't take one of the major league coaching positions you were offered."

"I would have loved those jobs. Or even the commentator jobs I was offered. But I don't want to live in the city and be known for nothing more than my failed career. I like kids."

They headed up the interior stairwell to Zander and Heather's enormous apartment above the clinic. They left their shoes on the top landing.

"If you like kids, why are you planning on moving away from them? And don't give me that crap you give Mom about making changes that count. Nothing gets changed below the state level and all of that happens in the city." He went into the kitchen and grabbed a soda for himself and a bottle of water for Ty who struggled for words.

"Think about it. You could bring a lifelong love of sport and fitness to all those kids by being a gym teacher and coach. You'd still be in Half Moon Bay, with us. And, most importantly, you could marry Quinn." He paused to sip his beer. "Honestly, nobody cares who she dated. Everyone knows her or knows of her. She's practically famous for her healing skills. She's a good choice."

"You think I don't know that? I do." He tossed the unopened bottle of water on the couch and watched it bounce back onto the floor. When he didn't cross the room to pick it up, Zander did.

"Dude. You're an idiot. You love her. Everyone in the family knows it. You have for months. You could barely keep her eyes off her for the past four years. When you had your rehab when she first moved here, she was all you could talk about. Admit your love. Propose, properly this time. Get married, have a minivan full of kids, and find the job that fills your heart."

"Easy for you to say. What do you know about it?"

"Everything. I fought my attraction for Heather for way too long. Plus, I wanted a city career. I only came home because you and Jacob were still in the city, Derrick was a disaster, and I didn't want Mom to be alone after Dad passed. Turns out Half Moon Bay is my perfect home and career."

Ty snorted. Everyone had such good advice, at least in their opinion.

"Listen to your heart. It knows what you want. Maybe the universe is sending you a sign that admin isn't for you?" He shrugged expressively. He sat in the recliner and raised his feet, then stared as if he was waiting for Tyson to have an epiphany.

Neither said anything for several minutes. Uncomfortable with his brother's silence, Ty sat on the couch. "Is there a game on?"

They watched a rerun of a Leafs-Panthers hockey game while they waited for supper. It was a good thing he'd already seen the game because he sure wasn't seeing it now. He stared at the screen and sipped his water while his mind whirled. His thoughts bounced with the uncontrollable rebound of a hastily tossed football, going this way and that, without heading in anything close to a straight line.

His career didn't even come close to the dominant thoughts. Quinn was first and foremost in his mind. Why had she rejected his proposal? It didn't make sense. He ran their last conversations over and over in his head.

It hit him like the epiphany Zander had seemed to be waiting for. He'd basically told her she was trash. No wonder she'd been so upset, though that wasn't how he meant it. Then, his proposal had basically said he was doing her a favor.

"I'm an idiot," he mumbled.

"No doubt there," Zander quipped. "Want to narrow it down for me?"

One thing about his family, he could always count on them to be supportive and sarcastic all at once.

"About Quinn. My proposal sucked."

"I told you that when you first got here. Women like all the bells and whistles."

"How would you know? You proposed by giving a woman who was afraid of animals a cat and doing it in public."

"I groveled. I put myself on the line, publicly. It proved I was serious and that I smartened up after being so wrong about not wanting to get married." His smile was soft for a moment before it turned serious. "Take the chance man. If you love her, do it right. And, if they fire you or refuse to give you the admin position, who cares? A happy home life trumps a crap job any day. Though, if you ask me, you'd be better off, and happier out of admin and working directly with the kids."

"I don't know about that." Slowly, his thoughts settled and came into focus. The distant idea that wasn't quite formed the night he was at Quinn's morphed into a plan. A life with Quinn and her baby, and more kids. Maybe he could go back to coaching. He would enjoy working directly with the kids. Technically, it was a step down from where he was now, but he didn't need the money. If he had, he might have considered coaching in the NFL when the jobs were offered.

Quinn was important to him. He finally admitted, at least to himself, that he loved her. He'd loved her for a long time. Over the past years, all their casual meetings and physio appointments had turned to attraction, and then to like, and now to love. He could picture her in his house, in his life. Sharing cooking chores, reading together, and making love. Walking the dog.

Wait. Dog?

Neither of them had a dog.

He wasn't opposed to a dog. How would she feel about one? It didn't matter. No new pets until their baby was older.

Yeah, their baby. It wasn't his genetically, but ever since he learned she was pregnant, the baby felt like his. It was the child of his heart. He had to stop calling the baby it. *What did she call it? Oh ya, Little Bean*. He already loved Little Bean.

His mother would be thrilled.

"I gotta go." He leaped up.

"Don't run off half-cocked. Do you have a plan? What are you going to do? What will you say? How are you going to impress her?"

"I have no idea," he confessed, flopping back down just as the doorbell rang.

"Pizza," his brother Derrick called from the doorway as he let himself in. "I was getting myself dinner since Sammi abandoned me. I heard them repeat your address and figured we might as well have dinner together." He set three pizza boxes on a veterinary magazine on the coffee table and looked at Tyson. "You're the reason my girl took off. You should pay for dinner."

What started as a depressing evening of moping turned into a riot of sarcasm and brotherly love when Jacob showed up grumbling that he'd been abandoned by his wife and that his daughter was making cookies with their mom.

Ty's mind never really left his problems, but he trusted himself enough to come up with a solution, and a way to propose that might be accepted.

"Anyone going to the Spring Fling dance this weekend?" Jacob asked. "Heather's got the contract for the nibbles. She's got a great lineup of finger foods and we've hired a group of high school kids to be servers. It should be fun. Nothing like a dance to get close to my girl. If she ever gets out of the kitchen, and if Mom will watch Ella."

"When has Mom ever refused time with her first grandchild?" Tyson asked making everyone laugh. "I have to go," he blurted and jumped up. He carried his plate to the kitchen and set it on the counter, just the way their mother had taught them.

"You're not going to do anything stupid are you?" Derrick demanded. "You don't want to screw this up."

"I'm not you," he sassed back. "I'm going home to make plans. You guys have to get your ladies to make sure Quinn comes to that dance," he said as he put his shoes on.

"Ask them yourself," Jacob said. "Nothing women like more than being involved in a romantic scheme." His tone was all affection and joking.

"I'll do that." He spun back toward them. "Remember that time Mom made us do that dance for the talent show?"

"No way," Derrick barked. "Never again."

The others laughed.

"It won't kill you," Tyson said, half begging. "You guys are in, right?" He looked expectantly at Jacob and Zander.

"Only because you're my favorite brother," Zander quipped causing a good-natured argument between the others.

Tyson headed out, secure in the knowledge that they'd help him with his plan.

"I'm not wearing the suit!" Derrick called down the stairs.

Chapter Twenty-Three

"This is the stupidest idea ever," Quinn grumbled slipping into one of the dresses Heather had brought her from Hawaii. "Why would I want to go to a dance?"

Sammi, Lexi, Ella, Beth, and Heather stood in her living room, talking to her as she dressed in the bedroom. Why in the world was Tyson's family so set on her attending the dance? They'd shown up with five dresses to try on. Each was loose and flowing and wouldn't rub against her growing baby bump. In jeans, she still wasn't showing, at least not enough that most people would notice. Naked, she had the slightest curve that she couldn't stop resting her hands on.

She talked to Little Bean all the time and played her classical music. She didn't know why, but she was convinced her child was a girl. Not that she cared either way. The old saying, as long as the child is healthy, rang true, at least for Quinn. She'd changed her fitness routine from jogging and yoga to dancing and yoga. With the warmer weather, there wasn't enough ice to worry about, but she was half terrified of slipping and causing harm, even though she knew the likelihood of either was slim to none.

"I grabbed these when I was in the city," Beth said, handing Quinn a package when she came out of the bedroom to get approval on the dress.

Quinn opened the bag. It held six pairs of maternity tights in different colors and patterns.

"I thought they'd come in handy. I can't wait to take you shopping for maternity clothing. They had the cutest tunics and leggings."

"Thank you. I appreciate the gift. They're perfect." She held up a navy pair of tights. "These will be perfect with this dress." It was a good thing she brought them. While she could just squeeze into her jeans, nothing else fit except yoga pants.

The dress came to mid-thigh and swirled around her in gentle folds. It was the exact navy of the tights and patterned with white and yellow daisies. It looked like a summer day. The colors flattered her skin and when she glanced at herself in the full-length mirror on the back of the apartment door, she was glowing. Her spirits rose for a moment, then crashed.

"I still don't know why you all insist on me going tonight."

"Because you're family," Heather declared. "Besides, there's a pro lacrosse team in town to practice at the rink, though I don't know why. They're a men's team, in their thirties. You might just meet a new man."

"I don't know if you noticed," Quinn snarked, "But I've been impregnated by one man and dumped by another. Men aren't high on my priority list right now." She winced. "Sorry, Lexi. I shouldn't talk that way in front of Ella."

Ella laughed. "We took sex ed in school. I'm in the know."

"Come on," Sammi teased. "A handsome man to dance with. He might just give you a way to forget your woes. I know dancing with Derrick, when I can convince him to dance, is always sweet heaven." Her sigh was blissful.

"You won't regret it. And if you want to come home early," Beth said, "I'm happy to drive you."

"I'll take my own car."

"Don't be silly. The parking lot is way too small, that's why the six of us are only taking two cars."

"That reminds me. I'm going to need to upgrade my SUV. It's so small it'll suck to put a car seat in and out of it. I better do that now."

"No!" Everyone cried at once.

"That's a tomorrow problem," Heather said. "Tonight's for fun. Now hurry and get ready. I can't wait to dance with Zander." She waltzed herself around the living room, skillfully avoiding the coffee table and the other women. "Let's blow this joint and dance. Besides, my staff will be wondering where I am. It's a good thing they're well trained."

Within ten minutes, despite Quinn's protests, Beth pulled up to the community center. Crowds of people were strolling toward the wide-open doorway. Music filtered outside and an elderly couple danced on the center's wooden deck. The song ended and the man dropped to one knee and clasped his hands together like he was begging.

"Oh, look at that," Quinn exclaimed, discreetly pointing toward them.

"That's Amos and Dot Walkershire. They met at a spring dance as young adults in England. He proposed the next year at the same dance. Even though they're in the U.S. now, he proposes every year at the dance. He claims it keeps their marriage, and them, young."

"That's so romantic." Her pregnancy hormones peaked, and her lip trembled. *Dang it and busted shoelaces! She was not going to cry over a proposal.* Coming here was a mistake.

"Come on," Beth urged, dragging her forward. "I hear a glass of wine calling my name. Who knows, maybe there'll be a handsome man for me to dance with. Several gentlemen asked if I'd be here tonight."

They strode through the twenty-foot-long foyer, toward a table collecting donations for the Children's Unit of the hospital. They both dropped a few bills into their jar and received a beaded bracelet made by a child. She recalled hearing something about the grade one and two kids making them as a fundraiser. How cute was that?

Shouts of laughter came from beyond the second set of doors where the dance was in full swing. She shared a smiling glance with Beth. Maybe this would be okay.

Inside the main hall, a local band filled the stage at the far end and played a George Canyon song. Couples whirled around the floor, dancing and laughing. Some sharing sweet glances. Children raced through the dancing couples, squealing with delighted freedom. The room was enormous with a large dance floor surrounded by clusters of circular tables where Spring Flingers sat and chatted as they took a breather.

So much pleasure and happiness in one place soured her mood. Jealousy climbed up her spine. She didn't belong here, not in her current mood. She turned to leave. She could walk home, it wasn't far.

Beth caught her by the elbow. "No, you don't," she whispered. "Give it half an hour. If you're not enjoying yourself then I'll take you home. Oh look, there's Stella. Let's go have a chat, why don't we?"

Her fingers dug in just a touch as she dragged Quinn forward. They skirted the crowd to the far end of the hall and sat with Stella and her family, Jeff, and two members of the front office staff. The table was crowded. Quinn tried her best to make polite conversation, but mostly she just nodded and smiled when appropriate. She was grateful when the band announced a short break. The dance floor cleared except for happy kids who redoubled their antics.

Servers in black pants and white shirts or blouses wandered through the crowd carrying trays of appetizers. It dawned on her that she didn't have a ticket for the event, and it was a fundraiser. She must owe Beth, or someone, for her ticket. She'd have to figure that out.

The mayor stepped on stage and gave a quick speech of thanks for supporting the hospital. "Congratulations to Amos and Dot Walkershire on their sixty-ninth anniversary." The roar of the crowd was deafening. "Now, without further ado, The Bellamie Brothers are here to entertain you."

Beth's grin was huge. Quinn searched out the rest of the Bellamie ladies and they were all wearing weird grins. Something was up.

A loud triple-rap sounded on the closed foyer doors. Two men leaped up to stand in front of them. They nodded at each other and flung the doors open.

Tyson stood in front of his brothers. All were wearing their wedding tuxes.

The crowd fell silent, and parents hustled their children off the dance floor. The four Bellamie men strode forward confidently and after a brief pause, music poured out of a Bluetooth speaker. It took her a moment to recognize *I Don't Want to Miss a Thing*, by Aerosmith. In unison, like they'd practiced a hundred times, they began to dance.

It was badly choreographed, and their lip-syncing was off, but it was amazing.

Quinn stared at the foursome of men dancing in the middle of the buzzing community center. No one laughed. No one interrupted or joined in. It was like a command performance by a professional dance troop. With Tyson in the lead and his brothers slightly behind, they danced their way from the rear of the room toward the stage. Derrick looked like he'd rather be anyone but where he was. Jacob and Zander had big grins, but Tyson looked nervous. Whatever in the world had prompted them to dance in front of the entire town? As they came closer, Tyson caught her eyes.

His smile was wide and nervous. Tears formed in her eyes. He was singing to her, for her. In front of everyone.

The song faded to an end with the dancers just four feet from her table. Tyson was in front of her, but his brothers slipped away into the silent crowd. He stopped moving and looked her straight in the eye. Without breaking eye contact, he stepped forward until he was two feet away.

Her heart fluttered.

Someone handed him a cordless microphone.

Her stomach dipped then rose alarmingly. What in the world was going on?

"Quinn Davidson, I want you to know that I'm an idiot. Totally blind and selfish."

Her mouth dropped open and she snapped it shut.

He paused for a moment as a light chuckle rolled through the crowd. "I thought my reputation was everything. I've worked hard to keep it clean and unblemished. Then you came into my world."

She frowned and the crowd gasped.

"Shoot!" he blurted. "I didn't mean it that way. I was a danged fool. I want to be with you. I've loved every moment we've spent together. You make me happy, though it took me a long time to admit that. I'm miserable without you."

She smiled just a touch as his confession eased the sting of his earlier comment. Her cheeks were hot, she was blushing. What was he up to, and why was he saying all this publicly?

"I am here to tell you something." Another pause. He swallowed twice, his Adam's apple bobbing. "I love you." He dropped to one knee in front of her. "Tell me I'm not too late. Tell me that you'll stay in Half Moon Bay and be my wife. That you'll let me be a father to your child. A child I already love. My heart is crushed thinking I've lost you both. We need to be a family. The universe put you here to show me a better way. My career isn't everything, my reputation isn't everything. Both are nothing without you. I'm nothing without you."

He set the mic down and pulled a black velvet box from his pocket. He flipped it open and held it up to her. A glittering diamond ring shone in the light. It wasn't flashy. It was a small diamond flanked by two rubies. It was exactly what she would have chosen. She stared at the ring, then up at him.

Words stuck in her throat.

He'd proven she mattered more than his reputation.

"Please," he whispered. "Don't leave me hanging."

She cleared her throat and swiped tears from her eyes.

"I'll take a no if I have to," he whispered. "But don't leave me here waiting. I can't stand the pressure." His lips barely moved.

She doubted anyone more than a foot away could hear him. This was what she wanted. She'd been wishing for this since their first meeting.

"How can I marry a man I've never even kissed? We might not be compatible."

He leaped up and swept her into his arms. His hands were warm on her cheeks. He looked deep into her eyes and said, "I love you, Quinn Davidson. I'm nothing without you. Please put me out of my misery and marry me." He swooped in, and brushed his lips across hers.

Lightning fired down her spine. Sweet heaven! She knew it would be good. But this exceeded all expectations. It was electric. Like a burst of passion and an incredible feeling of coming home.

He eased back and looked her in the eye before coming forward once more to capture her mouth in a real kiss. A deep, soul-revealing kiss. One that burned away her fears and resistance. He leaned her back, over his arm, and deepened the kiss.

The crowd cheered and clapped, the noise barely penetrating the delicious fog surrounding her.

Slowly, he brought her up upright and whispered, "Will you marry me?" against her lips.

"Yes." She murmured.

He leaned back and shouted, "She said yes!"

Pandemonium erupted and they were swamped with people congratulating them. The crowd separated them, but every time she looked at him, he was looking at her. Finally, he roared, "Let me through. I want to dance with my fiancée."

Dancing with Tyson was pure heavenly bliss. She was happier than she'd ever been.

At least until she heard a loud voice say, "How can he even think of marrying her, that baby isn't even his. I hear she doesn't know whose it is."

Tyson stopped abruptly and she bumped into him. "Wait here," he commanded and strode toward the voice.

He stopped in front of Mrs. Gilbert and in the next pause between songs declared, "Mrs. Gilbert, I don't care what gossip you may have heard, but this child is mine. You got that?"

"I heard it from a reliable source that it isn't." She crossed her arms over her chest and smiled triumphantly.

"I may not have conceived this baby, but from this moment forward, no from the moment I learned of the baby's existence, it was mine. It is mine. I love it like my own."

"How dare you speak to me like that? You will never have a job on the school board."

"That's okay. At the end of the year, I'm stepping down as principal. I've realized that I want to work with children. I'll be accepting the position of Phys Ed teacher and football coach. I have no desire

for a board position. I believe I can make more of a difference working with children."

"You won't get that job. I'll have you fired," she sputtered.

Tyson laughed. "Go ahead. I don't need the job. I'll open a youth
center, or help my future wife open her own physio business. There
was a day when your opinion mattered. That's over. All that matters
is my family and helping kids."

To Quinn's absolute shock, the woman stood and patted Tyson
on the cheek. "About time you grew some balls." She hoisted her
glass of wine. "A toast to the newly engaged couple."

The band started playing and Tyson was back at her side. "I love
you," he declared.

"I love you right back. I have since I first laid eyes on you."

Epilogue

"Are you sure you want to be here for this?" Quinn asked.

Ty drew her into his arms. "Absolutely. Like the song says, I don't want to miss a thing. Not one moment of this."

"Mrs. Bellamie, come on back." The ultrasound tech stood in the clinic doorway. They were married two weeks ago in a quiet ceremony at Jacob and Lexi's inn. She'd moved into Tyson's house, and they were busy prepping the nursery. Or rather, Ty was, he wouldn't let her help, but he allowed her to watch. His overprotectiveness was irritatingly adorable. Most mornings he woke her up by whispering their engagement song in her ear. She hadn't thought him capable of something so romantic, but he proved his love to her every day.

"Let's do this," Tyson said, dragging her forward.

"I'm nervous," she whispered. Today, she was exactly three months pregnant.

"Like I told you at our wedding. We'll handle whatever comes our way. Good or bad. Besides I have a good feeling about this."

His calm words steadied her tripping heart. "Okay."

The ultrasound took a long time. Longer than Quinn thought it would. "Is everything okay?" she asked. So far, the tech hadn't let them see the screen. She was nervous and excited to catch her first glimpse of their baby.

"Just hang tight. I'm going to get the radiologist in here for a moment. He likes to keep up on these things."

Her stomach plummeted to her toes. "I'm going to puke," she whispered when the tech walked out of the tiny exam room.

"Breathe, baby. You'll be fine. The baby will be fine."

A tall balding man in his mid-fifties strode into the room. "Mr. and Mrs. Bellamie, I'm Dr. Urquart. I'm just going to take a peek like I do for all our new mothers." He sat and used the wand to conduct a full examination. After an eternity he said, "Would you like to see your baby?"

"Is everything okay?" Quinn asked, her voice shaking. She was on the verge of tears.

He spun the screen their way saying, "There is one small hiccup. You're having twins."

"What?" It took several seconds for his words to sink in.

"Congratulations, you have two healthy babies."

"Oh, thank God," Tyson declared, echoing her feelings exactly.

"What?" she asked again.

Tyson grabbed her hand and kissed it. "Quinn, we're having two babies." He grinned at her.

"Are they boys or girls?" she asked, still rocked with disbelief.

"I can't tell yet. That's what took so long. We'll have you come back in a few weeks for another look. In the meantime, congratulations to you both." He wiped the gel from her abdomen and handed her some tissues. "You're free to leave. Take a moment to enjoy the news. We don't need the room immediately."

"Holy broken shoelaces," she muttered. "I'm not ready for this."

"We will be by the time my sons arrive."

"Sons? These are girls."

"Boys."

"Girls."

They laughed together. "I guess two babies explains why I was sick so early on and why it still hits me now and then."

"I guess so." He helped her sit up, though she really didn't need help. "Thank you for this. For forgiving me, for marrying me, and for these two wonderful babies. I love you, Quinn Bellamie. I became whole when I met you."

"I love you too."

His sweet kiss rocked her to her soul.

Note to Readers

I have to say that I love stories with secret or surprise babies. It's one of my favorite tropes, and twins just make things better. Perhaps because I have twin daughters. Like Quinn, I knew I was pregnant within days of conception and was sick for months.

Old Dude, I guess he was Young Dude back then, and I frequently battled over the genders of our babies, just like Ty and Quinn. We had an enormous whiteboard on the office wall. Every day I'd write GIRLS all over it. He'd come home from his engineering classes and change it to BOYS. It was a fun battle we both remember fondly.

I hope you enjoyed Quinn and Tyson's story, and the rest of the Half Moon Bay Series. Audrey and I have had a blast writing them for you.

About Katie O'Connor

B est-selling author Katie O'Connor lives in Calgary, Alberta, Canada. She married her high school sweetheart and is living her happily ever after. She is the mother of two grown daughters and is extremely proud of her five grandchildren.

She is the founder of The Write Chicks, a private romance writers' group set up with the sole purpose of supporting each other's writing career. Currently she is the past president of the Calgary Chapter of the Romance Writers of America and head of their mentoring group. In the past, she's been their secretary and has also served on the organizing committee for When Words Collide, a reader and writer conference in Calgary, Alberta.

Katie's career path has been long and twisted, with most of her life devoted to her family. She's been a waitress, chambermaid, cashier, store manager, as well as a lab and X-ray technician. She's been a small business owner and is an avid quilter and crafter.

She's dabbled in writing since high school because something drives her to create stories. She swears it's impossible for her NOT to write. Unsatisfied with one genre, Katie writes contemporary romance, fantasy/paranormal romance, and romantic suspense. Her favorite genre is sweet small-town contemporary.

She believes in all things magical, including dragons, fairies, UFOs, ghosts, and house pixies. But most of all she believes in love, romance, and hope.

Katie's Social Links

You can find Katie here:

Email: katie@katieohwrites.com
Mailchimp Signup: http://eepurl.com/Q2nRr
Website: https://katieohwrites.com
Facebook: http://www.facebook.com/katieohwrites
Bookbub: https://www.bookbub.com/profile/katie-o-connor
Link Tree: https://linktr.ee/katieohwrites

Books by Katie O'Connor

Coyote Creek:

Fall in love along with the uniquely entertaining residents of Coyote Creek. They're sure to steal your heart and bring you smiles, laughter, and tears. A contemporary, small-town romance series centered around The Flint family, their ranch, their friends, and neighbors.

A Lesson in Love 1

A Heart Torn Apart 2

A Secret to Shatter 3

A Melody for Christmas 4

A Surrender so Sweet 5

A Place Called Home 6

A Love to Rebuild 7

Coming Home for Christmas 8

Coyote Creek Box Set 1

Coyote Creek Box Set 2

Cherry Lake Fire Fighters:

Cappuccino Mugs and Fire Fighter Hugs

Matchmaker Christmas

A Silver Fox Christmas:

Welcome to Christmas in Valley Springs, the place that proves that the heart can still find love as you get older. Valley Springs is the home of the hottest silver foxes in Canada. Pop in for a while, read these heart-touching holiday romances featuring ladies and gentlemen in their fifties.

Their Christmas Heart

Their Christmas Love

Their Perfect Christmas

A Silver Fox Christmas Box Set

Hearts Haven:

Welcome to the friendliest small town you've ever visited. Come, sit for a while, enjoy a cup of tea. Quirky characters, heartwarming romance, and picturesque mountain scenery. Fall in love with Heart's Haven.

Building Trust

Running Home

Saving Grace

Heart's Haven Box Set

Three Moon Falls:

Welcome to Three Moon Falls, the home of the Hawk sisters, four talented witches each with a special gift. With their abilities to control fire, water, earth, and air, it's hard to remain hidden in the broom closet, but they're doing their best. Mundanes don't believe in magic, or dismiss it as coincidence, and that's how it should be.

But if the Hawks can't stop evil from taking over Three Moon Falls, someone's going to notice the paranormal goings on, and the universe will spiral out of control. Can they keep their magic a secret? Is it strong enough to defeat an evil entity with decades of experience, or will the sisters lose everything, including each other?

Water Magic

Fire Magic

Stand Alone Books:

Carly's Heart

Cupid's Charm

Hearts in the Spotlight

To a Tea

Bulletproof Heart

Fake Dating at Half Moon Bay

Gingerbread Dreams

Christmas in Silver Creek

Sleigh Bells Inn

Protecting Josie

Rekindled Fire

Books with Heat:

Corralling the Cowboy

Cornering the Cowgirl

Tessa's Trio

The Gift